2099 meltdown

BOOK 5

2099

meltdown

John Peel

BOOK 5

AN
APPLE
PAPERBACK

SCHOLASTIC INC.
New York Toronto London Auckland Sydney
Mexico City New Delhi Hong Kong

ISBN 0-439-06034-6

Copyright © 2000 by John Peel. All rights reserved. Published by Scholastic Inc. SCHOLASTIC, APPLE, and associated logos are trademarks and/or registered trademarks of Scholastic Inc.

12 11 10 9 8 7 6 5 4 3 2 1   0 1 2 3 4 5 6/0

Printed in the U.S.A.

First Scholastic printing, May 2000

For Richard Kusevich

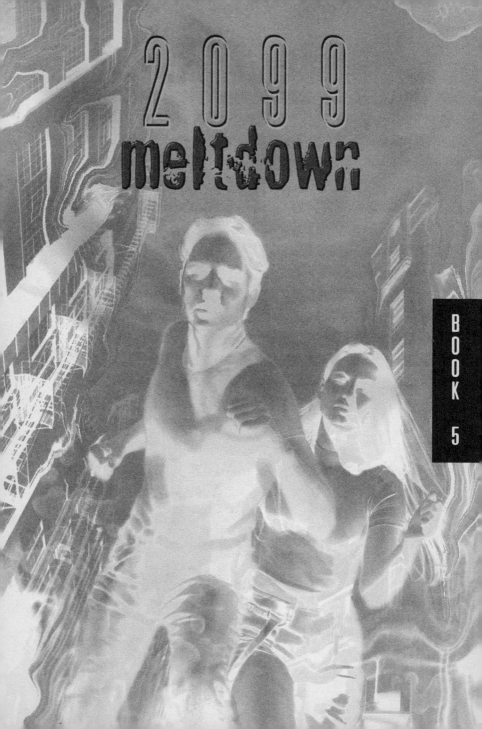

Prologue

It seemed to Tristan Connor as if everything had finally fallen apart. Just when it looked like he had managed to get all of his problems under reasonable control, a fresh, horrible problem had arisen. He looked into the smirking face of Marten Scott and realized that the man was not lying: He had set a trap for anyone unwary enough to try and access his computer. And it wasn't just any trap — it was the Doomsday Virus, which had already destroyed a great deal of New York City and killed thousands of innocent people.

The shields thought that Tristan had created the virus, and he was still on the run from them because of this. He knew he'd be able to clear his name, but only if he captured and exposed the real creator of the killer virus — his clone-twin, Devon. But he didn't know where Devon was, and if the virus was released again, the shields were bound to blame Tristan for it. When Devon first released the virus, Tristan had managed to stop it by using a special hunter-killer program of his own design, his stealth dogs. But Tristan couldn't pull the same trick again, because all of the stealth dogs had been destroyed. If the virus was released again, nothing would be able to stop it. . . .

Tristan glanced at Genia. The sixteen-year-old girl was a thief at heart, but she was a brilliant computer hacker and a pretty neat friend, even if she tried to hide it. She looked even sicker than he did, but she had every reason to be. This whole plan was the brainchild of the renegade organization named Quietus. It planned to destroy all of human civilization by eliminating Earth/Net. Transport, groceries, life-support systems, housing — even people's identities — they were *all* stored and controlled by WorldNet. If that should collapse, so would human civilization. Quietus was counting on this so they could step in and rebuild the world with themselves in control. Marten was not merely the Malefactor — one of the nastiest and sickest of the Quietus traitors — he was also Genia's father. Genia might be a thief, but she was appalled by the plans her father had made. She looked as though she wanted to beat his head to a bloody pulp against the nearest wall. Maybe that was exactly what she wanted to do. Tristan could hardly blame her — he was more than tempted to hurt the man himself, and he had never believed in violence as the answer to anything.

Next to Genia stood Barker. Tristan wasn't quite sure how he'd managed to pick up the biggest crook in the Underworld as his ally, but Barker and his partner, Lili, were proving to be very dependable in an odd sort of way. Barker was a predator, stealing from the world Above, and he knew that if Quietus succeeded in destroying WorldNet, it would destroy his livelihood as well. So he was working on the side of the angels for a change. Barker's fingers were clenching and unclenching, and the man was obviously picturing them around Marten's neck. Lili looked as if she was carved from a block of ice, but there was something fiery in the expression of her dark eyes.

Almost in the background, Mora was sitting down. She had once been Tristan's girlfriend, and he had thought that she loved him and trusted him. However, she had betrayed him to the police, thinking she was doing the right thing. Then her whole world fell apart. She and her parents had been sentenced to life in the

Underworld and thrown to the mercy of the animals — human and otherwise — who lived there. Mora had joined Barker's band to survive, and she now blamed Tristan for everything that had happened to her. She wanted revenge on him, and she refused to listen to his explanations. The past few days had revealed a terribly nasty streak in her nature, and she was looking forward to the time when she could hurt him physically as much as she was convinced he had hurt her emotionally. His eyes shied away from her and back to the gloating Marten.

"I guess the world ends about now," Marten said mockingly. "You know the shields have investigated Ice by now. They're bound to enter my cell, and when they see my Terminal, they're going to try and access the information stored in it. And when they do . . . bye-bye world!"

Tristan's throat had gone dry. He licked his lips, trying to think of what to do next. Marten was quite correct. The madman had gladly spent most of his life in jail on Ice, in the Antarctic, knowing that nobody would think to look for him behind bars. Thanks to his corrupt contacts, he had a state-of-the-art Terminal in his cell. The shields were bound to try and access it for information, and when they did . . .

"We have to warn Shimoda," Tristan finally decided.

Barker snorted. "As if she'd believe a word *you* said. After all, she's the shield who's been trying to arrest you. She still thinks that this is all your doing. If you tell her not to access that computer, she'll do it just to spite you."

Tristan's heart sank — he realized that Barker was right. Shimoda would never believe a word he said.

Genia moved forward. "I'll talk to her," she decided. "All things considered, she's not a bad person — for a shield. And she owes me a few favors by now."

"Will she believe you?" Barker asked. "You're a crook, too, don't forget."

"I worked with her for a while," Genia answered. "I think she'll listen to me. Anyway, I already sent her information that helped her. She's got a strong sense of honor — she knows she owes me."

"And she's also quite keen on seeing you back behind bars, I should think," Barker said. "You know shields — their first thought is always to lock people up."

"Shimoda isn't like that," Genia said. But Tristan could detect a note of uncertainty in her voice.

"It hardly matters whether she believes you or not," Marten said. "There's no way she'd be able to stop the shields from accessing my Terminal anyway."

"We have to try," Genia said. She moved to the hovercraft's control station and punched in Shimoda's private access code, which the shield had given her when they were working together. It seemed like a lifetime or two ago, but it was actually less than two weeks. In seconds, Shimoda answered the call, and her face twisted in confusion and, perhaps, other emotions.

"Genia," she said softly. "I've been wanting to talk to you."

"I'm sure you have," the thief agreed dryly. "But there's no time now to tell me what you think of me. Is there a shield force in Ice right now?"

Shimoda looked wary. "And if there is?"

"Tell them to stay clear of Marten Scott's cell. He's a member of Quietus, and he's rigged his Terminal to download the Doomsday Virus if anyone tries to access its files."

Shimoda went pale. "How do you know this?"

"Because we kidnapped him!" Genia snapped. "He's here with us, now, and he's boasting about what he's done. You've got to stop anyone from touching that Terminal, or the world dies!"

1

aki Shimoda had never asked to become Head of Security for Computer Control. It had been thrust upon her by her boss, Martin Van Dreelen, when Shimoda had uncovered the Quietus conspiracy. The former head, Peter Chen, had been sent to Ice as a member of Quietus. Now, however, Shimoda had come to believe that Chen had been framed by the real villain within Computer Control.

And her chief suspect was Van Dreelen himself . . .

It was one terrible headache after another. Shimoda had sent her friend, Lieutenant Jill Barnes, and a squad of shields she could trust to go to Ice and question

Chen with Truzac. The truth serum revealed what she had suspected — Chen was innocent, framed for crimes he hadn't committed. But she had also discovered that someone had beaten them to Ice and freed one of the prisoners, Marten Scott.

Now, if she could believe Genia, Shimoda knew who it was, even if she didn't know why. And if what Genia claimed was true, there was a greater disaster about to happen. Shimoda was a pretty good judge of character, and she was almost convinced that Genia was telling the truth. But only *almost* . . . Nodding, she turned from that conversation and brought up the link to her shield forces on Ice. "Stay with me!" Shimoda called to Genia. "We still have to talk."

"Stay with you?" Genia grinned. "So you can trace this call and arrest us? Sorry." She reached to shut down the link.

"You have my word this call is not being traced," Shimoda said urgently. "Please, just wait!" She didn't have the time to check to see if Genia believed her. Jill Barnes's face came up on her Terminal.

"What's wrong?" Barnes asked anxiously.

"Has anyone entered Scott's cell yet?"

"Chen's in there. There's a Terminal full of information he's attempting to access."

"Get him off it *now*!" Shimoda yelled. "It's rigged to

release the Doomsday Virus into WorldNet if anyone tampers with it!"

Barnes swallowed, paled, and nodded. She whirled around and dashed into the cell. Her comp went with her, of course, so Shimoda was treated to a dizzying view of the dash. The screen focused again on Chen at the Terminal, typing instructions.

They were too late!

The world was about to end. . . .

Shimoda's mind almost went into shutdown. She felt as if she was a million miles away from her body, completely unable to interact with the world at all. Sweat started trickling down her forehead and spine. She wanted to scream, beat her fists on her desk, *anything*, but she was locked there in frozen horror, staring at the Terminal and knowing it was all over. Dimly, she was aware that Barnes was yelling at Chen to get off the computer, that the virus was going out to destroy everything. . . .

It was all over. The vast majority of the human race was doomed. There would be a few survivors, but not many, once the world collapsed.

Chen was saying something. At first Shimoda's numbed brain refused to take it in. But then some of it got through to her. Her mind thawed out, and she discovered that she could move again. She leaned forward, staring at the Terminal. It hadn't melted down yet. . . .

"What?" she asked.

Chen's face loomed out at her. "I said I'm no fool. I disconnected the Net and isolated this machine before I began to access anything. It can't release any virus. In fact, there's no sign of any problems with the Terminal at all."

Relief washed over Shimoda like a flood. She remembered to start breathing again. "Chen, be careful with that thing," she warned him. "These people are very dangerous."

"Tell me about it," he said sourly. "I'm the one they framed and sent to prison, remember? And — what the —?" He whirled around, and dived for the Terminal he'd been working on. "The system's crashing!" he exclaimed. "The virus is destroying the computer!"

"But nothing else?" Shimoda was half begging, half praying.

"I told you, it's isolated." Chen worked feverishly, but the machine had obviously seized up. "Damn. The whole thing's melted down. We've lost the data."

"Including the Doomsday Virus?" asked Shimoda.

Chen nodded. "Including the virus. The whole thing's fried. We'll get nothing from it."

"Don't worry too much about that," Shimoda told

him. "The important thing is that the virus didn't get free. And that it's now destroyed." Something occurred to her. "And Quietus doesn't know that yet. They must think they've still got the virus."

"What are you planning?" Chen asked her.

"Seal down Ice," she ordered. "Lock up the prisoners. Scott may not have been the only member of Quietus there. I don't want any of the prisoners communicating with the outside world. Shut down any Terminals or phones in the prison area. Then keep the place sealed until further notice. I don't want Quietus finding out about the virus."

"Understood." Chen abruptly grinned. "Technically, am I reinstated as Head of Security? If so, you can't be giving me orders, you know."

"Believe me, I wish you were," Shimoda answered. "I'd be very happy to get out of this office and back to the beat. But I know Van Dreelen won't approve of you coming back yet. Let's just play it by ear for now, shall we?"

He gave her a mock salute. "You seem to be doing fine for now, boss. I'll get this place sealed up and then report back."

With relief, Shimoda minimized the transmission package from Ice, and brought back her link to Genia. Had the girl trusted her? Would she still be there, waiting? There was no way to be sure without attempting to restore the link. Somewhat to Shimoda's amazement, Genia was indeed still waiting.

"The virus is destroyed," Shimoda informed the girl. "It didn't get into WorldNet. My agents destroyed the link before it was unleashed. Only Scott's terminal was destroyed."

"Well, it's nice to see that you shields can do something right without me holding your hands," the girl answered. She was being sarcastic as usual, but Shimoda could see the relief on her face. "Still, I expect you'll be wanting more help anyway, right?"

"Something like that." Shimoda felt very uncomfortable. "Genia, I know you felt that I let you down when Chen had you arrested. But there was nothing I could do — at the time."

"Yeah, I kind of figured that out," Genia admitted. "I guess I'm not so mad at you anymore, otherwise I wouldn't be bothering to talk to you, would I?" Then her eyes narrowed. "What do you mean — *at the time*?"

"Things have changed," Shimoda replied. "I'm now Head of Security for Computer Control."

"Hey, maybe I should throw you a party."

"It means I'm now the one giving orders," Shimoda pressed on, ignoring the girl's hurting comments. "And I've given one, setting you free."

"Big deal," Genia scoffed. "I'm already free, remember. I broke out of your maximum-security jail." She grinned. "And then broke back in again and brought out my father."

"Your father?" Shimoda was getting used to Genia's delivery of surprises, but this was one that rocked her. "Marten Scott is your father."

"Biologically speaking, yes," Genia said bitterly. "Aside from that, he's a worthless piece of human garbage. I guess I'm the one thing he did right in his life."

"Yes, he did pretty good with you," Shimoda agreed. "But you don't seem to quite understand. You've broken yourself out of jail, but I've had you set free. The shields are no longer hunting for you. The charges and sentence have been dropped. Legally, you're a free person."

"Free?" Genia blinked.

"Yes. And I'd like you to come back and help me. I think you'd be invaluable at helping me break Quietus. What do you say?"

Genia went silent for a moment. Conflicting emotions played across her face as she struggled with the decision. That Shimoda trusted her seemed to mean a lot to the girl. But was it enough to overcome her natural suspicion of shields?

"And what about Tristan?" Genia finally asked. "Is he getting the forgive-and-forget treatment, too?"

"He's still our number one wanted criminal," Shimoda said gently. "He created this virus. Just because it's destroyed doesn't get him off the hook."

Genia sighed. "In which case — thanks for the offer, lady — but no thanks."

"Think about it a minute, Genia," said a voice from off-screen, one that Shimoda recognized well.

"Connor!" she exclaimed.

Tristan moved to join Genia on the screen. "Me," he agreed. He turned to the girl. "Genia, you should take her up on her offer. There's no need for you to be on the run, too. Go back."

"Are you trying to get rid of me, brain boy?" Genia snapped. "Sick of me already?"

"No!" Tristan protested. "But the inspector has given you want you want — your freedom."

"And she hasn't given you yours," Genia pointed out. "She still thinks you're the maniac behind all of this." She looked out at Shimoda again. "He isn't, you know. He's telling the truth — he really does have a clone, and it's that clone who's behind the virus. What will it take to convince you of this?"

What indeed? "The clone," Shimoda replied, trying to

sound firm. "I'm sorry, Genia, but I can't help thinking he's duped you. You should turn him in, so this whole thing can be resolved. I promise you, I will check into this allegation of a clone. And if Tristan is innocent, I give you my word he'll go free."

"Yeah, but *when*?" Genia asked. She shook her head. "Sorry, but I happen to think that the best way of beating Quietus is with Tristan. So thanks for the offer. If it's still open later, maybe I'll take it. But not until Tristan's been proven innocent." She shrugged. "Is that all?"

Shimoda was tempted to break her word and trace the call. To get Connor back in their hands again, and this time subject him to Truzac . . . That might be all they needed to destroy Quietus. But to do that, she would have to break her promise to Genia. And that wasn't an option. "Yes," she said sadly. "I suppose it is. I wish I could convince you."

"And I wish I could convince *you*," Genia echoed. "Maybe I'll see you later, when this is all over. Oh, yes — one last little present for you. Marten told us that he only knows the name of one other person in Quietus. It's somebody that you know pretty well, apparently. The name's Van Dreelen. Maybe you should do something about him." The screen went dead.

Shimoda sat back in her chair, stunned. If Scott was telling the truth, then he'd just confirmed her worse fears. Van Dreelen *was* a member of Quietus. But he was also one of the most important people on Computer Control. What could she do? Even knowing the man was a crook didn't help — she needed *proof* of his guilt. Neither Scott's nor Genia's words were enough.

But it definitely meant that she couldn't trust the man. Anything important that she did now would have to be done without his knowledge or approval. But how could she keep a member of the board in the dark?

She rubbed her temples. Her headache was coming back, and she didn't think she'd be able to get rid of it very easily this time. It seemed as though this new job of hers was going to destroy her health — mental and physical. She wished Genia had accepted that offer of a job. She could use the brilliant young hacker right now.

And what about Connor? Shimoda had once been absolutely certain that the boy was lying about having a clone, and that he had indeed written and unleashed the Doomsday Virus. But Genia seemed equally convinced that Connor was innocent. And Genia was no fool.

Maybe, just maybe, the boy was telling the truth?

If so, what did that mean? That there really was a clone of him somewhere out there. A very dangerous individual, the more so because he was hidden and unsuspected. Shimoda hesitated. Could she assume that she'd made a mistake simply because Genia thought so? It wasn't like she was always right!

Shimoda simply didn't know what to believe anymore. She only knew that there was a lot to be done, and almost all of it would have to be concealed from her boss. And that she would have to find evidence of his guilt.

Another day of sheer torture . . .

2

Jame Wilson glanced out of the airlock window and saw the dusty plains of Mars stretching toward the pink sky. For once in his life, the sight didn't make him think about the beauty of his planet. Instead, he thought how appropriate the reddish color of everything was. The reds spread from a light pink to a deep bloodred, and that seemed so right, given what was happening.

War, on the planet named after the god of war. It might have been funny if it wasn't so real and terrifying. Jame wasn't scared for himself as much as he was scared for everyone else he knew.

His father was in the Administrator's prison for having tried to stop the madness. Jame had always disliked the Administrator, but now he actively loathed him. The man had brought in shields from Earth and used them as shock troops, calling for martial law and a curfew. He'd provoked a strike by the spaceport workers, and then had the shields kill some of the strikers, pretending that they were part of a rebellion that needed to be put down fast. The Administrator now had control over the seven cities of Mars, with his own, corrupt shields enforcing his laws. But the *real* shields, the Martian ones under the command of Captain Montrose, refused to let this happen without a fight.

Montrose had declared that the Administrator was corrupt and had to be removed. Almost all of his shields had backed him up, and that meant Montrose was leading a real rebellion. Jame, his mother, and his baby sister, Fai, had all joined Montrose. So had a lot of the other Martians. On the whole, Martians were an intelligent bunch of people, and they could see that what the Administrator was doing was wrong.

And now the whole situation had escalated into war.

Montrose's aim was quite simple: to remove the Administrator and shut down the shields loyal to him. The Administrator, of course, wanted to do exactly the same thing to Montrose. The problem was that this was unlike any war ever fought before. Aside from the fact that there hadn't been a war on Earth in thirty years, there had never been one in space, and certainly never one on Mars. In a war on Earth, for example, both sides might try blowing up sites held by the others.

On Mars, that was unthinkable.

The problem was that if *anything* breached the walls of the cities, it could kill everyone inside. The natural atmosphere of Mars was far too thin for anyone to breathe. Only inside the cities could people breathe normally without air suits. Outside, a person would gasp for breath and die in minutes. They would die in the same way if anything cracked the walls of the cities. So there was an unspoken truce in this war with the Administrator: Neither side would blow anything up. It would do Montrose no good to remove the Administrator but kill everyone in the city while doing so.

Even shooting off guns anywhere near a window might break the glass. It was very tough glass, but nobody really knew whether it would stand up to gunshots. Most of the shields were armed with tazers, of course, which fired electrical bursts instead of bullets. If these bursts hit a person, they would either knock that person out or kill them, depending on the setting of the gun. The problem was — what if a burst hit a control panel? A surge of electricity might short-circuit the controls. Then what would happen? Maybe the air regenerators would shut down. Maybe the heating elements would stop working, and the temperatures on Mars would freeze people in a short while.

So even the use of tazers was carefully watched. It was a strange sort of war, with neither side actually shooting at the other one much. Thus it was a war where Jame was invaluable.

He was a brilliant hacker, the best on Mars. And whoever controlled the computers controlled Mars. The computers ran everything, and the Administrator, theoretically, controlled the computers.

But Jame was aiming to change all of that. While Captain Montrose and six of his shields watched for trouble, Jame opened up a wall panel in the maintenance bay. He couldn't get at the main Terminals directly, since they were in the administrative offices and under the control of the other side. But if he had the access, he could take command of MarsNet from anywhere. With his desk-comp, he had the ability to hack in, provided he could do it through a good access point. Montrose had deduced that the one in the maintenance bay was their best bet. Since all space flights to Mars had been canceled, the bay was sitting idle. The usual crush of workers getting space ships ready wasn't there. The men and women had been sent home and the area sealed off.

It had taken Montrose and his shields less than five minutes to break the seals to get into the bay. Once inside, Jame had set to work. With the wall panel off, he had access to the crystal flow network that carried all of the computer's commands and information. Jame plugged his comp into the unit, and set about tracing the electronic pathways that kept Mars running. He tried to focus on what he was doing and ignore the shields, but that wasn't always possible. They were men and women used to action, and sitting around quietly waiting wasn't what they were good at. As Jame hacked his way into the command pathways, the shields checked out the maintenance bay.

They found something odd in the Terminals there. One of the women, Lise, called Montrose over to her. Jame was working, but he could hear what was going on.

"According to these records, Captain," she said softly, "not all ships have been sent away. There's a flight plan shown for a single vessel from Earth. It should be leaving in the next twenty-four hours and making a fast trip out here. Real fast."

"Why?" Montrose asked, puzzled.

"Reinforcement shields?" one of his men suggested.

"No," Lise said firmly. "That was my first thought, too. But I don't think so. I've been checking the records of the shields that the Administrator already has. Normally, they'd all be assigned from one office on a job like this — London, probably, or maybe Vancouver. But this bunch were taken from all over the world. One from Cairo, a couple from Tel Aviv, one from Buenos Aires — that sort of thing."

"Maybe the Administrator thought it would be less noticeable?" Montrose suggested.

"I think there's a simpler reason," Lise argued. "I think these shields he brought in are pretty much all he could raise that would be loyal to him. Let's face it, it couldn't be easy to find a lot of shields who would ignore their oaths to protect civilians and to be loyal to Computer Control. I don't think he has any more troops he can call in. The ones he's got here now are all that there ever will be."

"Well, that's encouraging, if you're right," Montrose said. "But if there aren't any reinforcements, then what's that ship for?"

"The Administrator's bosses," Jame answered. "Quietus. The ones who sponsored this whole mess."

Montrose was thoughtful for a minute. "It makes sense," he agreed. "They're coming here to take command. But surely they realize they're bound to be found out? I mean, Mars may be pretty much independent of Earth, but I can't imagine Computer Control just sitting around and letting a terrorist group take over Mars."

"Nor can I," Lise agreed. "So I'd say they're probably going to fix that before they leave Earth. They'll have some way to ensure they won't be stopped."

"They'll sabotage EarthNet," Jame said firmly. He glanced up from his own work. "I've been looking over the reports from Earth, and there was some kind of virus that virtually wiped out New York City, and the name of Quietus came up attached to it."

Montrose whistled. "If they sabotage EarthNet, then Earth will have too many problems of its own to be bothered about what's happening up here on Mars. It's just nasty enough to work. But what can we do about it?"

"About EarthNet?" Jame shrugged. "Nothing. We can't even access it directly from here. Whatever Quietus is doing, Computer Control is going to have to deal with."

"Can't we warn them or anything?" Lise asked. She sounded concerned.

"How?" Montrose asked bitterly. "Communications are all routed through the Administrator's office. Even if Jame can hack into them, it won't help, because we don't have the power to transmit a message to Earth."

"We have to deal with our own problems," Jame said

firmly. "And trust that Earth can deal with theirs. They're not stupid back there, and Computer Control does know about Quietus." He finished his wiring. "There. I've got my comp linked into the Net now. All I have to do is to hack into the computer controls and rewrite all of the passwords. With luck, we can shut the Administrator out of his own Terminal, and then he'll have no power to control anything. Once we're in command, I can shut down the air supply to the shields and the business offices. That should force them to surrender in a hurry."

"Fingers crossed," Montrose agreed.

"But I'd appreciate a bit of quiet for the work," Jame added. "It's kind of draining."

"Understood. We'll shut up now." Montrose nodded to his shields, and they moved to cover the entrances and exits from the bay.

Jame focused on his Terminal and began work with his speedboard. There were safety measures built into all of the programs, of course, that would theoretically guard against what he was aiming to do. But they were written by only very good programmers — and he was far better than that!

He hoped . . .

He typed away, fingers flying and mind racing. It was

like playing a very complex computer game. He had to wear down the programs and guards, step by step. It was hack, capture, neutralize, discard . . . and then begin again on the next level.

Jame had no idea how long he worked. He was concentrating entirely on his task. He'd managed to get through the first levels of encoding, and was sneaking in the back door of the power plant when he was suddenly aware of problems.

There was a yell, and then a burst of noise. An explosion? His ears rang, and he looked around.

No mistake — they were under attack! The incoming shields were shooting off everything they had, apparently not at all bothered about the damage they might do. Jame couldn't believe it.

He also couldn't stop. He was too close to getting what he wanted. If he pulled out now, the Administrator's programmers would be able to repair his breaches and prevent him from trying again. He had to keep going while there was still a chance. The problem was that there was a chance he'd get shot, too. . . .

He spared a quick glimpse and saw what had happened. Montrose's people had guarded against the enemy shields coming at them from the city. But the other forces had come from the void outside, wearing minimal body armor and breathing masks. They couldn't have survived more than ten minutes outside in such spare equipment, but if they'd run from the other airlock to the one here, they could have made it in time. Once inside the airlock, they'd opened fire on Montrose.

Already a couple of the shields were down. Montrose's forces were dressed in traditional black outfits, while the Administrator's replacement team wore blue with gold piping, so it was easy to tell the two sides apart. Jame noted there were more people in black down than there were in blue and gold.

"We've got to fall back!" Montrose yelled. He tapped Jame's shoulder. "Come on."

"No!" Jame snapped. "I'm almost there. I just need a couple more minutes, and we'll succeed!"

"We don't *have* a couple more minutes," Montrose growled. "They outnumber us, and we're getting hammered." A blast from a tazer seared the wall ten feet away, underlining his remarks. "We've got to go."

"You go." Jame was sweating. There was a sick feeling in the pit of his stomach, and he knew it was fear. But he couldn't give in to it. One more layer to go . . . access, analyze . . . "I'm finishing the job. The codes you'll need to access control are on my mom's wrist-comp."

"I'm not leaving you!" Montrose whirled and fired. One blue-and-gold went down in a heap.

"You've got to." Jame was almost there now. It was hard to ignore the blasts and the screams as people were injured, but he focused his mind. "You're distracting me."

Montrose made a move to grab his arm, but another tazer blast slammed into the wall overhead. Montrose jerked back, and then realized he didn't dare try to grab Jame again. They'd be too good a target together. "Idiot!" he snarled. Then, to his shields, "Pull back! Now!"

Jame ignored them. He typed in the last commands, and the control panels were open to him. He sliced out all of the old command codes and installed his own overrides. Then he sealed off access, to prevent any of the Administrator's puppets from overwriting what he'd done.

The Administrator no longer controlled the power plant. And once his mom accessed the computers, she would.

Time to go . . .

He ripped his desk-comp from the wall, and turned to run.

Three of the blue-and-golds were there. One of them raised a tazer. For an awful second, Jame saw everything clearly. The officer, his eyes focused solely on Jame; his finger tightening on the tazer's control; the barrel of the weapon pointed directly at him.

The lethal setting on the gun . . .

Jame screamed, pulling up the comp to shield himself as the man's finger finished pressing the trigger and the tazer erupted with electrical death.

The blast enveloped him. There was a brief second of absolutely horrible, unendurable pain.

And then nothing.

3

Devon was getting increasingly annoyed. He had expected his role as master of the Moon to be a whole lot of fun, and he was disappointed. He paced back and forth in the old Net broadcasting station he'd taken over as his base of operations in Armstrong City, the capital of the moon, glaring furiously at the monitor screens.

Devon had been raised away from all other human beings, looked after by 'bots who fed and reared him. His only human contact had been the Malefactor, whom he had never even seen face-to-face, only via VR. Not that Devon felt any need for any other humans, of course — he'd have to be slumming to associate with them. But their tawdry, dull lives were sort of interesting. He enjoyed watching them go about their mundane existences.

Once he'd taken over command of the Moon from its weak and pliable governor, he'd discovered that the Lunar dwellers didn't believe in security monitors such as they had on Earth. And that meant Devon couldn't watch people. He'd promptly ordered the governor to install monitors in everyone's homes. There had been some protest at first, but the installation had been completed. True, people were getting very annoyed with the governor for forcing the monitors on them, but that didn't bother Devon at all. The man was an idiot, and deserved all the grief he got.

What *did* bother Devon was that the Lunies were not simply obeying their orders.

He glared at the wall of Screens, each of which should have held pictures of dull, boring people living their shallow, empty lives. Instead, all of the Screens were blank. Some people had painted over the lenses of the cameras. Other had simply covered the cameras up, tossing things like hats over the lenses. In every case, Devon got nothing worth seeing.

Furiously, he'd ordered the governor to deal with the situation. The moron had simply sent shields around to uncover the cameras. Naturally, as soon as the shields left, the stubborn inhabitants covered over the cameras again. What did the governor expect?

Devon sent through a signal to the governor's office. The overweight, sweating man stared back at his master. He looked properly terrified, but Devon was no longer amused by this show of fear. "You're not handling this situation very well, Governor," he complained. He gestured at his Screens. "I'm still not getting any pictures. And that makes me angry. You know how short a fuse my temper has."

"What can I do?" the man bleated, spreading his hands. "The people hate the new law you forced me to pass, so they're fighting it."

"Then you have to show them that they can't win this fight," Devon said, spelling it out for the man. "Throw a couple of them in prison; that should wake the rest up."

"In prison?" The governor went paler than normal. "On what charges? No court on the Moon would let me do that."

"Who cares *what* anyone else will let you do or not?" Devon yelled. "*I'm* running things now, and you'll take my orders or else pay for disobedience. And you know what I can do." He'd been forced to kill a squad of shields the governor had sent after him; the lesson had proven to be very effective.

"You don't understand," the governor complained. "I run things on the Moon, yes. But there are legal limits to my powers. The courts can rescind my orders — and there are already lawyers arguing for the repeal of the monitoring law. It's not going to survive a legal challenge, you know."

"You idiot," Devon growled. "You don't have a clue what *real* power is, do you? Laws in books, voters in the streets — they mean *nothing*." He flexed his fingers in front of the Screen. "With these fingers, I can kill every last person on the Moon. *That's* power! I'm the only one here you should be afraid of. *Very* afraid of. Forget the courts, because I can overrule them all. The shields are nothing. The wishes of the people are nothing."

"It's not that simple," the governor protested.

"No, you're wrong — it *is* that simple. And I'm going to prove it to you. I'll take no more disobedience. From now on, people will learn that they obey me or else they die; the choice is *that simple*." Devon smiled. "Everyone here on the Moon is alive only because I graciously let them live. Well, my patience has limits, and it's time to show everyone what will happen if those limits are reached." He turned to the blank Screens. One was from the Monro domicile. "Monro!" he called. "By order of the governor, uncover your camera lens."

"By order of the governor?" The picture suddenly

came back. "You know what I think of the governor?" The man made a rude gesture and then covered the camera again. "Get lost."

Devon was smiling, but he shook his head and sighed. "That's a *really* bad attitude you have there, Monro," he said. "We can't have you being so disrespectful to our kindly governor. Since you won't live well, I think it's time you stopped living at all." He typed a command into the Terminal. "There we go. Doors sealed, and the air's cut off."

There was a moment's pause, and then Monro's shocked voice. "What are you doing?"

"Giving you a choice," Devon said cheerfully. "You can either obey the law and uncover your camera — or else you can choke to death on your own defiance. Think about it, but don't take too long. According to my calculations, your air will be unbreathable in thirty minutes."

"You can't do this!" Monro howled. "I'll report you!"

"To whom?" Devon mocked. "Communications have also been cut off. You get your air and power back only when you stop being a criminal and start obeying the law. Uncover your lens, or die. It's a very simple choice."

Monro started yelling out curses, so Devon cut the audio link. "Dear me, some people are *so* stubborn, aren't they, governor? Now, let's see who's next. Ah, Bella Took . . . Hi, Bella," he called out. "It's Judgment Day. . . ."

Devon worked his way down the first twenty defiant Lunies, while the governor wept and pleaded with him to stop. Devon would have shut him off, but it amused him to see the man coming apart like that, so he let him whine. All of the Lunies yelled and cursed, but they wouldn't do that for very long. They'd give in, or they'd die. Either way, their protests would stop.

"That's the way you rule, governor," Devon explained. "This little problem will be over very shortly."

"You're crazy!" the fat man answered. "You think people will just take this without protest? They may cave in to your blackmail, but they'll start InstaSuits and get the courts on their side."

"Yes, I can see that they might make your life a bit of a problem," Devon agreed without sympathy. "Tough. Nobody really loves politicians anyway, you know. But it's *you* they'll hate, and that's nothing to me. If they decide to elect you out of office, I couldn't care less. Whoever they vote into your place, I'll still be in control."

"You're a monster!"

Devon yawned. "You're getting rather dull, you know. You've called me that before. Jeez, can't you think of any *inventive* insults?" Then he raised a hand. "Hold that thought. I'll have to get back to you. I seem to have somebody coming to their senses."

It was Bella Took. She looked as if she was having trouble breathing, but she had removed the blockage over her camera. "Okay!" she choked. "Now turn on the air."

"You didn't say *please*," Devon chided her. "Didn't your parents teach you any manners?"

"Please!" the woman screamed.

"There, that wasn't so hard, was it?" Devon turned back on her air and power. "Now you can breathe again. And the governor will kindly let you breathe just as long as you be good and obey the law. The next time you try covering your camera, the power and air goes off and it stays off. Do you understand me? This was a one-time offer only, and won't be extended."

"I understand," the woman said, venom in her voice. Well, it would be directed against the governor, not Devon, so Devon didn't care.

"That's the spirit. Cooperation is the keyword. Oh, excuse me, I think I have another applicant for my mercy. . . ." He turned to Monro's screen. The man was in bad shape, gasping for breath, his face already blue. His hand was shaking badly, but he managed to uncover the camera. He was gasping out noises that were obviously meant to be words. "Whoop! Sounds like you're having trouble interfacing." Devon mocked. "Well, I see that you've changed your tune a bit. Or you would, if you could sing. Now, I assume this means that you'll behave yourself from now on? Choke once for *yes* and twice for *no*." Monro gasped, clawing at the camera. Devon sighed. "I suppose I'd better take that as affirmative." He switched back on the man's air. "But this is your last chance, Monro. Next time I leave you to die. Ah, I think I have another caller. . . ."

The rest of the rebels caved in faster than Monro and Bella Took. Devon finally switched them all back on again, and considered starting over with another twenty. He decided against it. For one thing, word of this was bound to spread, and the others would probably come around without needing to be attacked. Also, he was getting bored with this game. You could only watch so many people panting for fresh air in one day. Maybe he'd start again in the morning, if he felt like it.

Devon smiled brightly at the governor. "There you go," he said. "A practical demonstration of how to handle problems. You could learn a lot from me, you know. If you were smarter."

"Learn?" The governor spluttered. "You almost killed those people!"

"And I got them to obey the law, didn't I?" Devon

shrugged. "It was their choice all along. I just helped them to make up their minds to be law-abiding citizens. Now, you go off and play. I've got work to do." He turned his attention away from the Screens and went back to surfing the Net.

He was a bit disappointed and annoyed with Quietus. It was *days* since he'd escaped from their custody on Overlook, the space station orbiting Earth. He'd really expected the Malefactor to be hot on his trail long before this. Didn't the man realize how valuable Devon was? It was rather insulting that they didn't have all of their forces out hunting Devon down. Not that they could catch him, of course — but he was rather disappointed that they didn't even seem to be trying.

He hacked into the Malefactor's private line, knowing this was a little dangerous. If Quietus found a link to the Moon, they might come after him. But Devon was getting bored playing by himself. He needed a bit of a challenge. Besides, he'd thought up some nice new ways to infuriate his cyber-parent.

To his amazement, the Malefactor's Terminal was down. He investigated more, and his eyebrows rose. "Not down," he muttered to himself. "Fried." What was going on? There was only one possibility he could think of: Tristan, his dumb clone. The other boy was pretty good with computers. This had to be his handiwork.

Devon was amused; it served the Malefactor right, having to deal with that kid. And it kept Tristan away from Devon, which was nice. On the other hand, Tristan was proving to be somewhat better at playing these games than Devon had expected. One of these days, he decided, there would have to be another showdown. When he had the time to spare, of course. Right now there were more important things to worry about than his clone brother.

There was a disturbance on the governor's Screen. Moss, the governor's assistant, had entered the office. Unseen by them, Devon watched, curious. What was going on?

Moss looked very angry as he marched over to the governor's desk, where the fat man sat. "I've had several complaints," Moss snapped. "The shields have been informed, and I have to tell you that they're drawing up charges against you now, Governor. How could you possibly authorize the use of force against your own people because of those stupid cameras?"

The governor was sweating, as always. "I didn't authorize force," he protested. "Things just got . . . out of hand."

"And now they're getting into court!" Moss yelled. "I always knew you were a politically minded moron, but I didn't know how low you'd stoop when things went against you. I'm warning you now, I'll do everything I can to bring you down over this matter."

"I can't say I blame you," the governor answered. "But it won't make a whole lot of difference to the colony, I'm afraid."

"What are you talking about?" demanded Moss. He looked confused. Devon was irritated; the governor was obviously going to tell the man all about Devon. Well, let him; what harm could it do?

"There's a monster behind all of this," the governor said. He gestured at the wall camera. "He's probably watching us right now. He has control of the computers, and has threatened to shut down the heating, power, and air all over the Moon if I don't obey him."

Moss's eyes narrowed. "Are you crazy?" he asked. "Do you think I'd believe a mad story like that?"

"It's true," the governor said miserably. "There's nothing I can do to fight him. He's the one who made me pass the law about cameras. And he's the one who almost killed people over it."

Moss stared at the governor. "You're pathetic," he said finally. "You won't even take responsibility for your own actions. You make me sick." He marched to the door and then turned back. "They'll probably be here to arrest you shortly."

"Thank you," the governor said meekly. Moss made a disgusted noise and left the room.

Devon laughed, and then opened up a link to the governor. "That didn't go too well, did it?" he mocked. "They don't even believe that I exist. They'll throw the book at you."

"I'd sooner be in prison than be party to any more of your evil," the governor said in an unusual show of temper. "At least I'll be away from you."

"Don't be silly," Devon informed the man. "I had cameras placed in the prison first of all. I'll be able to watch you perfectly well in there. And deal with you, if I feel like it. There's no escape from me." Still laughing, he cut the link and settled back to think.

Losing the governor was no big deal. Maybe Moss would replace him. Moss looked like a much more interesting man to break. It could be fun.

Except . . . Devon shifted in his chair. To be honest, he was getting restless here. The Moon was a bit too easy to control. It wasn't really a challenge any longer. He pulled up a picture of Earth, as seen from the lunar surface. The half-globe hung above a crater wall, blue and white and quite pretty. *That* was where Devon should be, taking command. Not here, hiding away in an overgrown tin can. The Moon was getting dull and stale, like the recirculated air. Devon had to be off again, taking over his destiny — Earth.

But he couldn't do that as simply as he could threaten the Moon. Oh, he could take over Computer Control and run almost everything. But he would never have the control over Earth that he had here. He couldn't control the air that people breathed or the water they drank . . .

Or could he?

He checked out the space ships, which were either in dock in the cities or else in orbit around the Moon. There was trouble on Mars, caused by Quietus. Devon knew that Quietus aimed to escape there when they wrecked Earth, and were turning away all other Mars-bound ships. Some had come to the Moon, others to Overlook or back to Earth. And among those ships were a couple that Devon could find a use for.

What he needed was a way to force Earth to surrender to him. And he was pretty sure he'd found it when he checked the loading manifests for the ships in the docks. An ultimate weapon that the shields couldn't stop, one that would make him Master of the World . . .

Of course, he'd deal with these obnoxious Lunies before he left them for good. They had irritated him, and that meant they had to be punished. *Severely* punished.

He knew just what to do.

4

Shimoda paced around her office again. When she was a child, she'd loved going to the Bronx Zoo. There she'd seen a tiger pacing about in its holo-enclosure, and she'd wondered why such a powerful creature had been walking up and down, eternally restless. Now she had some idea: Maybe he, too, felt trapped — not by physical barriers but by mental ones.

What was she going to do about Van Dreelen? Without proof of his guilt, she was stuck, and she had only the words of criminals saying that he, too, was one. She needed evidence, and the only place she could get that was from his computer records. These records were legally sealed against her, unless she could get a court order to force Van Dreelen to open them. The problem there was that at least one judge had been working for Quietus. If Shimoda went to the wrong judge, she would be the one in trouble, not Van Dreelen.

Meanwhile, what could be done about Quietus? Shimoda now knew three people who belonged to it — Judge Montoya, who was in jail herself; Marten Scott, who was the captive somewhere of Genia and Tristan Connor; and Van Dreelen, who was untouchable. Montoya had been given Truzac, and she had told everything she knew about Quietus's plans. Shimoda had skimmed the record, and seen that Quietus aimed to flee Earth and then release the Doomsday Virus. This would cause the collapse of EarthNet, and that, in turn, would destroy most of the human race. Hospitals, airports, cities, homes — all were tied into EarthNet. If the Net collapsed, so would everything else. Food production would cease; medical help would fail. Emergency services wouldn't be able to move. Flitters would stop. Cities would die. Homes would lock. New York City had shown how dangerous this was — thousands of people had died, locked in their apartments, the first time the Doomsday Virus had escaped.

The only good news was that the virus no longer existed. Once Scott's computer melted down, there was no more Doomsday Virus. Without that, Quietus could never strike.

An idea hit Shimoda with sudden, absolute clarity. She thought about it for ten seconds, then hurried to call Chen on Ice. If she was right, maybe they could get the proof they needed and finish Quietus once and for all. . . .

Chen's face looked back from the Screen at her. "Something wrong?" he asked.

"Just a thought," Shimoda replied. "Quietus aims to flee to Mars. They think that Scott will then release this Doomsday Virus when they notify him. They don't know we have Scott and that the virus is destroyed. How much information did you manage to get from his Terminal before it melted down?"

Chen grinned. "I think I get your idea. And the answer is that I got enough. I'll have another Terminal installed, and sign on with Scott's passwords and account information. When Quietus tries to contact him, they'll actually reach me."

"Wonderful." Shimoda felt as though things were finally going her way. Maybe her idea wasn't so crazy after all. "When they contact you, agree to release the virus on their command. They will then signal all of their members to leave Earth and head into space, where they will rendezvous for the flight to Mars."

"And you'll be waiting?"

"Don't I wish!" Shimoda shook her head. "I'm not sure I can swing that. I'm still calling for volunteers to take Truzac and prove their loyalty, but it's an uphill battle. Most of the officers think it's degrading to be interrogated like that. Most of them are probably loyal — they just don't want to have to prove it. And that means I can't trust them. I don't know if I'll be able to assemble a space assault team to get Quietus or not. I'm praying I can. But at the very least, we'll be able to identify the traitors in Computer Command."

"That's your play," Chen said. "I'm rather glad I don't have to deal with it." He grinned. "I'm enjoying not having to make all the decisions, you know."

"Don't get used to it, you rat," she warned him. "I have absolutely no intention of staying in this job one second longer than I have to. As soon as you're back here, you get it back again."

"Why do you think I wanted to stay on Ice?" Chen grinned at her again and signed off so he could get to work. Shimoda smiled. She felt so much better knowing that she could trust him again. It was wonderful having at least a few people she could be absolutely certain of; for a while, she'd felt so alone in her battle.

She called for Tamra, her secretary, another one of her loyal workers. When the woman came in, Shimoda explained what was happening — even though it was likely that Tamra already knew, since she had a habit of eavesdropping. "What I need you to do," Shimoda finished, "is to wait till we hear from Chen. As soon as we know the time that Quietus is gathering in orbit, send a message out in my name to every member of Computer Control. Tell them there is an emergency meeting convened for an hour after that time, and that everyone who possibly can make it should be there physically. Then, when the meeting starts, I want you to trace where all the hologram attendees are being transmitted from."

"And if they're from orbit, they'll be the Quietus traitors," Tamra said, catching on. "Gotcha, boss. I'll make it my absolute priority. We'll nail the lot of them, I promise you."

"I really hope so," Shimoda said. "But I have a nasty feeling that they'll have more tricks up their sleeves. Van Dreelen, for one, is ferociously brilliant." She frowned. "Speaking of him, do you know where he is? He hasn't been around all day, which is unusual. He hardly ever leaves the administration building. And he hasn't bugged me for a dinner date, either."

Tamra nodded. "He seems to have a crush on you, chief."

"Let's see how he manages a dinner date with me when he's on Ice," Shimoda said grimly. Van Dreelen was quite attractive, but knowing he was a criminal made all the difference in the world.

"I'll see if I can trace him," Tamra promised. Then she smiled mischieviously. "I think I'll accept a dinner date on your behalf, and see where and when he'll suggest. That should give me time to trace his call."

"You Web-rat!" Shimoda was going to object, but Tamra hurried out of the office, laughing.

Now Shimoda had to face her next problem: what to do about Mars. Shimoda hadn't been following the Newsbots too closely, since she was so busy, but she had heard something about civil unrest. It couldn't be a coincidence that this was happening just when Quietus was planning to flee there. She moved to her desk and called up all of the recent records on Mars. She had to understand what was happening there, so she could formulate a plan.

Technically, even though she was Head of Security for Computer Control, she didn't have any authority on Mars. Mars was an independent planet, with its own law enforcement division, courts, and politics. But she could alert the authorities there and have them take action. As she scanned the files, a very uneasy feeling grew within her.

The news reports out of Mars were very sketchy — there was a bit of a clampdown on the media, it seemed. But there was a measure of civil unrest going on, and some of it involved the shields. She scanned this part with more attention. It seemed as though the local shields had rebelled against the Administrator. That sounded awfully suspicious. Quietus must have infiltrated the shields there as they had on Earth and was using them to try and take over Mars. Luckily, the Administrator seemed to be getting the situation into hand. Maybe Quietus wouldn't have anywhere to flee. . . .

Then Shimoda realized something. If the shields had rebelled against the Administrator, how was the man managing to win the fight? Nobody else on Mars was armed. . . . She pulled the records and then started sweating. The Administrator had brought in shields from Earth to contain the trouble — but he'd asked for the troops a week *before* the trouble began. And the orders assigning the shields had been signed by Van Dreelen. Neither she nor Chen had seen the requests.

It stank. Shimoda sat back, concentrating. The shields on Mars weren't leading a revolution — they were fighting back against a corrupt Administrator! The man had raided the shield forces on Earth for Quietus agents willing to do his bidding.

This made things a lot harder. She couldn't just ask the Administrator to arrest the Quietus members when they arrived on Mars, as she'd been hoping to do. The man was on their side. That meant that if Van Dreelen and the others could make their escape to Mars, they'd be free. And that was unacceptable.

She checked the records of the shields sent to Mars, and saw that they'd been taken from different units from all around the planet. That gave her hope. Van Dreelen had pulled out most of the shield traitors to use on Mars. There couldn't be a lot of Quietus operatives left on Earth now. Or so she hoped.

Shimoda called Schwarzenegger Spaceport in Newark and ordered three Ramjets prepared, and assigned crews to them all. Then she had the duty officer assemble teams for each ship and hold them ready for action on her command. If she could only discover where the traitors were in orbit, she'd have her teams attack and capture them.

Finally! Action — and an end in sight.

There wasn't much more she could do until Quietus chose to make its move. Once it did, her trap would spring into action and hopefully it would close around all of the traitors. Somehow, though, she doubted it would be that simple. With people of the caliber of Van Dreelen on the other side, she had to be ready for surprises.

With a little time on her hands, she turned her mind to the final problem that was bothering her: Tristan Connor.

Maybe Shimoda had been too hasty in dealing with him? In which case, she had better start checking on Tristan Connor. If the boy *was* innocent, then there really was still a madman running around somewhere. Normally, she would have considered this very idea insane — but she'd seen so much these past days that she no longer could be certain what was and wasn't possible.

So — how to check the story? Well, the most obvious method was to see if she could find any evidence of a clone. She knew that there had to be *some* illegal cloning going on. After all, she had run into the young clone of Computer Control's own Dennis Borden. She didn't know if the old man knew about the clone, and she couldn't force a man that powerful to take Truzac and submit to questioning. But there was another way of tracing things . . .

She put a call in to Dr. Emili Dancer, and it was promptly answered. Even one of the world's best-known medical researchers knew to answer a call from Computer Control. The woman was in her late sixties, Shimoda judged, with a shock of white hair that contrasted with her wrinkled, ebony skin.

"Doctor, I'm sorry to disturb you," Shimoda apologized. "I'm sure I've dragged you away from something important."

"You are, are you?" Dr. Dancer snorted. "Well, you'd be wrong. I was playing a Space Krash IV. What do you want?"

"I have reason to believe that an illegal cloning laboratory exists," Shimoda explained.

Dr. Dancer snorted again. "I could have told you that," she complained. "I know of at least three. So what?"

The doctor was obviously not the easiest person in the world to get along with, but she might be an invaluable help. "A young boy of about fourteen claims he has an identical clone," Shimoda continued. "Do you have any idea how I might go about investigating such a claim?"

"Simplest thing in the world," Dr. Dancer replied. "You don't know much about cloning, do you?"

"Only that you can make sheep without fathers and that it was decided to outlaw any experimentation on human beings."

"Child's play," Dr. Dancer answered, waving her hand airily. "And the business about no experimenting on humans is stupid. It's born of fear, not wisdom. But when people are involved, decisions tend to get taken on a gut level rather than a brain one. Anyway, there are definitely places doing illegal cloning research. You can't stop scientific curiosity by telling people not to do things. Scientists will simply find a way around things. We're insatiably curious, otherwise we wouldn't be in this business."

"Can we cut through all this chatter to a simple answer?" Shimoda asked her. "Do you know how I can check if there is somewhere that may have cloned a boy?"

"Simplest thing in the world," the doctor repeated. "Look, cloning is like any other manufacturing process — everybody has their own method of doing it, and they try and keep their own ways from being copied by other people."

Shimoda was starting to get the idea. "Sort of like copyrighting a story?" she suggested.

"Exactly. So, if you had a DNA sample for me to check, I could probably tell you who made it."

Shimoda nodded. "I have two samples," she answered. She had Borden's clone DNA on her files, plus the DNA taken from Tristan. "Will that help?"

Dr. Dancer held up her hand. "Not so fast!" she snapped. "I said I *could* tell you where the clone was made, not *would*. You seem to forget that these people involved are likely to be friends of mine. I'm not just going to betray them to you because you asked me nicely."

Shimoda winced. "I suppose pointing out that they are technically criminals isn't going to sway you? And that hiding evidence about criminal activity is a criminal action in itself?"

Dr. Dancer snorted again. "Throw me in jail, then."

"I don't want to throw you in jail," Shimoda said, exasperated. "I just want to find out if this boy is telling me the truth that he's a clone. If so, he's innocent of a crime, and his clone-twin is guilty."

"That's more like it!" the doctor said, rubbing her hands together. "Good twin, bad twin, eh? Sounds like fun."

"I'd hardly call it that." Shimoda called up the data and transmitted it to the doctor. "How long would it take you to tell me whether these two people are clones, and where they were likely to have been grown?"

"The first part I can answer immediately." The doctor pointed at the pictorial representation of the dead man's DNA. "This man's quite clearly a clone. Look at the sequences here." Then she shrugged. "As if you could figure it out! Take my word for it, this man is definitely a clone."

Shimoda knew that, of course. But she'd sent the

Borden sample simply so that she could test the doctor's skills. "And the other one?"

"Is far, far more interesting," Dr. Dancer answered, excitement gleaming in her eyes. "This isn't a direct cloning, I can tell that."

"So he *isn't* a clone?" Despite her own beliefs, Shimoda was rather disappointed to find that Connor had been lying. She'd started to hope he'd been what he claimed.

"Did I say that?" the doctor snapped sharply. "I said he's not a *direct* clone, young lady! By which I mean that his DNA wasn't simply taken from another person, stuck in a jar, and grown into a new body. But he's a clone alright. Very, very nicely done. Can't be more than six or seven people in the world who could have done a job like this. And one of them is me, so that reduces it to five or six. Lovely work — not that you could appreciate it. He's a new-bred."

"A what?" Shimoda was getting more and more lost with the woman's report.

"His DNA isn't taken from any one person. Whoever made this boy worked hard at it. There are fragments of DNA codings from at least six other people spliced together here." Dr. Dancer was entranced. "He's obviously been selectively bred, for some purpose. Just what, I couldn't say until I analyze this more fully."

"Try being a computer genius," Shimoda suggested.

"I *am* a computer genius," Dr. Dancer said haughtily.

"No, I meant that was what the boy was bred to do." Shimoda chewed her lip. "Could there be more than one of him?"

"Almost certainly," the doctor agreed. "If you're making someone this complex, you'd need a few backups, in case anything went wrong. And to check the breeding patterns, to make sure everything goes as planned. If I'd been doing it, I'd have created at least ten of them."

"Ten?" Shimoda was appalled at the thought of even more of the computer maniacs out there.

"Well, I wouldn't bring them all to term," Dancer answered. "But I'd certainly raise two or three. I'd be very surprised if there weren't others just like this boy out there somewhere."

So Tristan *had* been telling the truth, then! Shimoda felt horribly guilty. She'd simply assumed he was the murderer, and hadn't listened to him. Well, she could make up for that later. "Can you tell me where the boy was made?"

"It'll take a bit of doing," the doctor answered. "This is important?"

"Vital," Shimoda assured her. "The virus that killed New York was created by one of those clones. I have to track him down before he releases it again."

Dr. Dancer scowled. "Then you have my full support. My younger brother died in his apartment there. I want to nail the people responsible. I'll get to work and call you when I have any results." She clicked off the connection without saying good-bye.

Shimoda sat back in her chair and considered what she'd just heard. She'd have to find Tristan and talk with him. She'd done him a terrible injustice, and would have to set it right. But finding that killer twin of his was more important right now. Quietus might not have the virus, but that boy could re-create it at any time. She *had* to get hold of him before he could do that.

Her desk-comp chimed, and Tamra's face floated in front of her. "News, chief," she said grimly.

"Just what I need — more bad news." Shimoda sighed. "Okay, what is it?"

"I've found Van Dreelen," her secretary announced. "He's definitely not going to be attending your meeting in person. He's already on Overlook."

On the space station? Shimoda was slightly stunned.

He'd already fled.

5

Tristan looked at Genia, at a loss for words. Finally, he managed, "You should have accepted that pardon, you know."

"Maybe I should have." Genia shrugged. "But, you know, I didn't think you'd manage to survive without my help. For all of your brains, you're hopelessly naive." Tristan was pretty certain she was only pretending that it was no big deal to her.

"Thank you," he said.

Genia grimaced. "If you're going to start getting mushy, brain boy, I may reconsider the offer. Anyway, what do we do now?" She stared pointedly at her father as she asked this. "You think we should turn him over to the first shield we come across?"

"They'd also try to arrest us," Tristan pointed out. "And we don't know if the shields will be able to hold him. They've been infested with Quietus agents."

"Well, I suppose we could always kill him," Genia suggested. For the first time, Marten's complacent look vanished.

"You little savage," Mora snarled. "You can talk about killing your own father?"

"I can talk about a lot of things," Genia said cheerfully. "But in his case, I think I could probably do it, too. In case you've not been paying attention, dimwit, he abandoned me as a child and has tried to kill me a couple of times these past few weeks. I really don't think I owe the scum any loyalty, do you?"

"He's still your father," Mora insisted.

"She's right," Marten added. "I *am* still your father."

"Keep reminding me of that, and I *will* kill you," Genia promised. "I'm ashamed enough already."

Tristan broke in. "I think that Mora's right; we can't kill him. That's not the way we do things."

"Speak for yourself," Genia answered.

"Isn't it nice to see everybody getting along so well?" Marten asked nobody in particular.

"Besides," Tristan said, ignoring the man, "he's not

our main problem right now. Devon is. I hope the shields can handle Quietus, because I'm sure we can't. But they'll never be able to deal with Devon. Only I can do that, because I'm as smart as he is, and I've got a couple of secret weapons."

Genia raised an eyebrow. "Wow. Super-spy all of a sudden, are we? And what are those secret weapons that have turned you into the savior of the world?"

"First of all, Devon doesn't know where we are, but I've a pretty good idea where he is. That gives us the advantage of surprise. And the other thing is that I have you on my side, and he doesn't."

"Awww . . ." Genia said, pretending to blush. "You say the sweetest things."

"I think I'm going to puke," Mora muttered.

Barker uncurled himself from the chair where he'd been listening to the conversation. "So, where is this killer kid, then?" he asked.

"I'd be interested in knowing that, too," Marten added. "I did rather lose track of him."

"He's on the Moon," Tristan said firmly. "Logically, he has to be."

"Logically?" Lili shook her head. "In other words, you're guessing."

"No," Tristan insisted stubbornly. "Look, he *was* on Overlook. That's where he" — he gestured at

Marten — "brought him up. I traced him there and tried to capture him, but he'd just fled. There hadn't been any flights to Earth, so he couldn't have come here. That leaves Mars and the Moon as possible places for him to go. He knows that Quietus is aiming to take over Mars, so he's not likely to head there. That leaves the Moon."

"It's a bit thin," Mora protested. "He might expect Quietus to take him back again, so he could be heading for Mars."

"That's not Devon's way," Tristan insisted. "But we can check on it. Wherever Devon is, he's bound to have hacked into their systems. Since we share the same DNA, I should be able to trace him and access his current plans."

"That sounds reasonable," Barker agreed. "But it's not something I'm going to be joining in with, I'm afraid. I think I've done about all I can for now. The virus is finished, and the main threat to my livelihood is gone. I wish you kids all well, but I'll be going home now."

"Besides which," Lili said, a smile twitching at the corner of her lips, "he's terrified of space travel. There's no way you'll ever get him up in a rocket."

"Oh." Tristan had never imagined that someone could be afraid of space, but he could see that Lili was telling the truth. "Well, Mr. Barker, thank you for everything you've done. We wouldn't have managed this without you."

"Don't get too sentimental, kid," Barker growled. "I only helped save the world so I can continue to rob from it. Enlightened self-interest and all that." Then he grinned. "If either of you is in the Underworld again, stop in and see us. You know where we'll be." He glanced at Marten. "And if you're off into space, you don't want to haul that deadwood around with you. I'll take him with me and keep him out of mischief. If he doesn't behave himself, I'll deal with him permanently."

"That would be a big help," Tristan said gratefully. He really had no idea what else he could do with the man. There was no doubt he needed punishing, but he didn't agree with Genia's idea of killing her father. He was far from sure that she really meant it, anyway. She had just been trying to strike back at him.

Barker looked at Mora. "What about you, kid? Technically, you're supposed to be working for me, but if you'd rather go off and save the world, I'll consider it vacation leave if you like."

Mora looked surprised. "You wouldn't mind me staying with them? And what about my parents?"

"I'll see they're looked after," Barker promised. "Go and do the heroic stuff. Maybe you'll even earn yourself a pardon, too, and get back to that nice house and lifestyle you once had."

"I don't remember anyone saying we wanted her along," Genia said sulkily. "After all, apart from betraying her boyfriend, what skills does she have that we need?"

"We could do with all the help we can get," Tristan said mildly. He didn't want the two girls fighting, but that seemed to be the way they were. "But if she does come, I'll want the two of you to get along."

"What do you think this is, a picnic?" Genia snarled. "I'm not getting along with that traitor, and that's final. How about I simply promise not to kill her?"

"That's a start," Tristan agreed. "Mora?"

"I'd like to come along and help," Mora said. She looked down. "I . . . have really messed things up so far. I want to make it up to you, Tristan. I want to do something right this time."

"That's good enough for me," Tristan said firmly. He glared at Genia. "How about you?"

Genia sighed and rolled her eyes. "I guess it has to be," she grudgingly admitted. "Since you seem to want her along. I just hope you're not thinking of kissing and making up with her. I might vomit."

Tristan flushed. He *had* been wondering if that was

what Mora had in mind. He didn't know how he would feel if she did try to get back together with him. She *had* betrayed him, but she had thought she was doing the right thing. And they had been going out for two years — two very enjoyable years. He couldn't figure out what he really wanted out of all of this. Plus, there was Genia to consider. She was two years older than him, of course, and said repeatedly that she had no romantic interest in him. But she seemed to be awfully jealous of Mora, so maybe Genia wasn't telling the whole truth? He simply didn't know, and his life was complicated enough without having to make romantic decisions right now.

"Well, if that's all settled, then," Barker said, rubbing his hands briskly together, "we'll be off. Good luck, and try not to get yourselves killed. You." He gestured at Marten. "On your feet, and behave. The first time you do anything wrong, my men will break one of your bones. I'll let them decide which one. The second time you annoy me, they'll remove some portion of your anatomy. An ear, a finger or something. The third time, they'll kill you. You'll soon wish you were still on Ice. That was the easy life." He threw Tristan a mock salute, then led his small procession out of the hovercraft and into the streets of the Underworld.

Lili stopped at the door, the last to leave. "Good

luck," she called. "I'm sure you'll do well. Earth's in good hands." Then she left.

"Earth's in deep trouble, in that case," Genia muttered, turning to Tristan. "Hey, this place looks bigger with just the two of us and her in it."

"Knock it off," Tristan grumbled. "We've got to get to work finding Devon."

"You said he was on the Moon." Mora was obviously puzzled.

"The Moon's bigger than you seem to think," Genia commented. "We need to narrow down the places to look just a tad. Right, Tristan?"

Ouch! Tristan hoped his nerves could stand this. "Pretty much so, yes." He started the hovercraft's built-in computer tracing.

"I'm aware that *somebody* is going to think me ignorant," Mora said. "But how can you find him on the Moon? I thought you couldn't access LunarNet from Earth."

"Technically, you can't," Tristan agreed. "But I never let little things like that bother me. This is a shield Terminal, and I'm using one of their secured lines to operate on." He'd stolen the access code from Inspector Shimoda. "I'm tapping into Overlook's security system. From there, I bounce a message to one of the communications satellites orbiting the Moon. Then I patch into

LunarNet from the satellite. It's stretching the link a bit, but it should be stable."

Genia locked in her own comp. "And while you do that, I'll run exactly the same thing to MarsNet. Maybe Devon isn't there, but who knows what we might find?" Her fingers were flashing as quickly on her speedboard as Tristan's were on his own.

"I feel so useless." Mora sighed.

"Gee, *that's* unusual," Genia commented. She subsided when Tristan glared at her. This wasn't going to be a very amiable party, obviously.

Concentrating, Tristan broke through the shield security, and hopped onto the communications satellite. That took a little more work, but it was basically simple encryption and decoding. Then he linked the final stretch, and was in LunarNet.

Now came the hard part. Devon would want to be hidden, and he was a genius. But he did share Tristan's DNA, and that meant that if Tristan could get a whiff of where Devon was, he could have few secrets that would stay hidden. The trick was tracking down where Devon might be. Tristan scanned recent news, pretty certain that Devon wouldn't stay hidden for long. His twin loved to meddle, and that was bound to leave some sort of a mark.

It took him less time than he expected. There was

trouble brewing in Armstrong City. It seemed that the governor had ordered monitor cameras installed in private domiciles, and that had caused a lot of unrest among the fiercely independent Lunies. Then the governor had ordered protesters attacked until they had given in. Impeachment hearings were under way.

It all smacked of Devon. "I think I've found him," he announced, calling the news item onto the main Screen.

"Why do you think that's him?" Mora asked.

"Because when I was in his rooms on Overlook, he had a whole wall filled with monitor Screens," Tristan said. "He was using security cameras to watch people. He seems to get a kick out of feeling superior to everyone else. This thing about installing monitor cameras on the Moon sounds like just what he'd want to do."

"How does that help us find him?" Mora asked.

"I can log in to the lines that are feeding the monitor images back, and get into the main computer system." He was doing it as he spoke. It called for access codes and a password. Not a problem, since his own worms were good at sorting out such things. The main problem was the time lag. It took two seconds for radio waves to travel from Earth to the Moon, and two more to come back, so there was a delay every time he sent instructions. Still, he could live with it, and his probes were working well.

"Got him," he breathed, a smile starting slowly on his face. "It *is* him. He's taken over an old NetNews center, and encircled it with his guard programs. But I recognize them. Now that we know where he is, we can go and get him."

"Can't we just tell the shields and have them arrest him?" Mora asked.

"He's too dangerous for the shields to handle," Tristan said. "If he gets any idea they're after him, he could do an incredible amount of damage. Right now, he's controlling the power, heat, and air on the Moon. If he shuts them down, people will die. And he *will* shut them down, if he feels threatened. If I'm there, I could start them up again, but nobody else can. Anything he can do, I can undo."

Mora nodded. "Then I guess we go to the Moon. I always wanted to take a vacation there anyway."

"Right. I'll just get us some tickets on the next shuttle." Tristan set to work. This was easy stuff.

"Um, guys . . ." Genia looked up from her board. "I think I just hit what is called a complication."

"Huh?" Tristan was confused. "On Mars? Is it Quietus?"

"I don't know," she admitted. "But I just found your

DNA trace again. Unless Devon's on Mars and on the Moon at the same time, I don't think you're twins. I think you're triplets."

"What?" Tristan moved to stare at her screen. The face of one Jame Wilson looked back at him. The same face he saw in every mirror . . . "It says he's been there since he was a child. You're right — there *is* another one of me. . . ." He felt numb. "Where is he?"

"Well, that's the problem," Genia said hesitantly. "This is his rap sheet. He's in jail. It seems that he's some kind of guerilla."

Tristan stared at the picture in shock. *Another* clone — and, it appeared, just as criminal as Devon was . . .

Was he fighting a losing battle? If both of his clone brothers were evil, what chance did Tristan have of being good? Maybe he was fooling himself, and it was only a matter of time until his own true nature came out.

Maybe the fact that he, too, was a wanted criminal wasn't simply a mistake.

Maybe it was his destiny.

6

Devon whistled happily as he drove the small electric cart through the corridors of Armstrong City. He was dressed very realistically in a repairman's uniform, and looked every inch the worker on his way to an important job. Of course, there was no real need for him to do any of this physically — he could have managed what he had in mind perfectly well enough on the Net — but he was discovering that there was a certain joy in doing things in person. Plus, he got to wear a disguise and pretend to be normal. The cart and uniform were borrowed untraceably from the workers' station nearby, along with all of the electrician's tools. This was fun.

He sounded the chimes to warn people to get out of his way. Honestly, he didn't care if they got run over, but the person he was pretending to be would care, so Devon acted the part. "Coming through," he'd call. "Mind the way!" Most enjoyable.

"Why are you so happy?" one man asked him as Devon passed by. "Haven't you heard what's happening?"

"I'm just doing my job, sir," Devon replied, smiling inwardly. "No time for the news. What's happened?"

"The shields have arrested the governor, that's what," the man explained. "He's to stand trial for almost killing hundreds of people."

"They should just shoot him," Devon suggested. "Save the city some money and the bother of listening to a load of politician's lies."

"True enough," a woman agreed, having overheard their conversation. "What's the Moon coming to, when you can't trust your elected officials?"

"What indeed?" asked Devon. "Sorry, got to be off. Can't sit around all day talking." *Unlike you, it seems,* he thought. Well, let them talk. They wouldn't have much more time left to enjoy it. Sounding his alarm, he set off again.

His first stop was the power station. Like all lunar cities, Armstrong had a central power core, a cold fusion reactor that bred power. It was very efficient and very safe . . . as long as nobody messed with it. Whistling happily, Devon promptly messed with it. He clamped a small comp into place and hardwired it into the system. Using the command codes taken from the central computer, Devon programmed his little device. When he sent the signal, the comp would switch command circuits. The central computer would be frozen out of the picture, and Devon's sabotage would begin. The comp would change the intermix for the core, causing the temperature to rise. Once it hit four thousand degrees, the place would go up like a bomb. This would shut down all power to the city, as well as turn about a quarter of the city into rubble when it exploded.

Armstrong City would die in a blast that would be visible even back on Earth. A nice touch. Devon had calculated where it would be visible, and set the explosion to take place when the Moon was high in the sky, to give everyone a good view.

The other cities were patched into this comp as well. Thanks to Devon's sabotage, all of them would experience exactly the same problems. All the reactors would blow up, one after another. Rather like a fireworks display.

By midnight tomorrow, the Moon would be empty of

all life, and there would be several very new and highly radioactive craters. That would teach these miserable nobodies to protest about Devon's policies! They'd all be nice and private in their graves. Except they probably wouldn't even have graves. Just a ruined city, pulled down over their stupid little heads.

Well, the Moon would be dealt with, but that was only a part of Devon's plans. Next he had to take over Earth.

With the Doomsday Virus dead, Quietus wouldn't be able to take control of anything. And Devon had no intention of ever going back to them and recreating it. He could do it, of course, but it would take time. Besides, repeating the same thing over again was boring.

No, now was the time for something different, something more interesting. But just as lethal. He had found just what he needed in the shipyard, getting ready to take off in a few hours.

Whistling and sounding his horn again, Devon drove his repair cart down the corridors to the dock. There were plenty of people around, most of them happily discussing the fall of the unpopular governor. Apparently his aide, Moss, had taken over and ordered the withdrawal of all monitors. The idiots in the corridors and meeting places all seemed happy, like they had won some great victory. They didn't have a clue what was *really* happening around here.

One young woman called out to Devon: "Come on! Take the afternoon off! Haven't you heard the news? The governor's in jail!"

"Take the afternoon off?" Devon made himself sound shocked. "Young lady, don't you know how *important* my work is? Got to keep things running smoothly. If somebody can't get a shower just when they want it, I'll be in real trouble, you know."

The girl laughed. "Don't be so serious!" she advised him. "Why don't you buy me dinner somewhere nice? Then we could go dancing. It's time to enjoy life."

While you still have it, Devon thought. He looked her over critically. She *was* rather good-looking, he realized. If you were into *touching* people like that. The thought of dancing with her, or seeing her physically eating was quite nauseating. She was so far beneath him, it made his head swim. "Sorry. Some of us have to keep the Moon running. But you enjoy yourself, and spare a thought for us poor workers while you do, okay?"

"Deal," she agreed with a theatrical sigh. Then she ran off to accost somebody else.

So that was what other people were like? Ugh! The concept of *mingling* with them was sickening. He was so glad that he was quite alone.

He drove onto the docks, and into the bay he was after. The cargo ship berthed there was old, but serviceable. It had to be thirty or more years old, and was showing it a bit. It didn't have much to do, though — just up and down from Armstrong City to lunar orbit. There it would pass its load on to a larger ship, one that was built to fly through space. The larger ship would take the cargo to Earth, where it would pick up more from another transport. Then it would head into the solar system, toward the Sun, where it would eventually get close enough to be drawn into the solar glare and melt.

It was, after all, a very good way of getting rid of the unwanted radioactive waste produced by the reactors. People had once buried this stuff on Earth, polluting it for centuries, if not millennia. Burning it up in the Sun was a far better way to dispose of it.

Only this particular load wouldn't be going anywhere near the Sun. Devon had need of it.

Though people oversaw the whole process, the main ferry ship was entirely computer controlled. It was simpler that way, so that no humans needed to be evacuated before the ship plunged into the Sun. And if the ship was run by computers, Devon could easily take it over.

It didn't take him very long at all to hack another comp into the system and subvert all of the command codes. Nobody would know that anything was amiss until Devon took over the flight plan when he was ready. He sealed the hatch he'd been working in, and that was that. A signal from him, and the ship would be under his control.

Everything was going very well — of course! Devon was so much smarter than these fools, how else would it go? Even if people believed the governor when he said that he had been forced to obey the orders of a boy, by the time the shields actually got around to looking for Devon, he'd be long gone — and the shields and everybody else here would be dead.

It couldn't be more perfect. The last thing to do was to get off the Moon before the big bang that killed everyone. That wasn't a problem, since there were plenty of ships still docked here. The only question was: Which one should Devon steal?

It had to be a craft that one person could operate. He didn't like the idea of having a crew around to cause complications, and there wasn't anyone else he could trust. That eliminated all but six possibilities right away. Of the six, four were out, simply because they were small one-person prospector ships. These were built for deep-range expeditions into the asteroid belt, where the pilot would then look for usable rocks with valuable minerals. The prospector ships tended to be pretty basic, with none of the little luxuries to which Devon was accustomed. He wasn't going back to Earth in a garbage scow — he wanted something with a little class.

That left two ships. The first was really tempting. It was a rather neat little ship built for racing. Some idiot was going to use it to try to break the Earth-to-Venus speed record. It had some of the luxuries that Devon enjoyed, but the problem was that it was due to leave in two hours, which meant that people would be swarming all over it still, getting it ready. Plus, there would be Newsbots there, covering the launch. For some reason, people seemed to admire fools who engaged in such spectacular attempts at killing themselves. Devon could have worked out a plan to get around all of these problems, but it wasn't really worth it. Not when he took a look at the final ship.

This was the one! It was a luxury one-person craft with everything Devon wanted. Best of all, it was the shield commander's private ship. There was a wonderful sense of irony about stealing a craft belonging to the highest law-enforcement official on the Moon! Plus, there was the little extra bonus that if anything should go wrong, the man would hardly give the order to shoot down his own ship.

His mind made up, Devon deleted all of the commander's controls and took over the ship's onboard computer. Then he ordered the craft to be fueled and prepared for launch. He faked a flight plan showing the ship as going to Mars, and then authorized it with Moss's private codes, hiding the transaction carefully.

Devon smiled happily. Everything was going wonderfully. Soon he'd be on his way back to Earth in utter triumph, and these stupid Lunies who had defied him would all be dead.

It was a good day.

7

Jame's whole body ached, but he knew he was lucky
to be alive. Even if that wasn't going to continue for
very long. The comp he'd been carrying had taken
most of the tazer blast, and had been wrecked. But
enough had been left to knock him out and leave him
with tingling nerves when he awoke. He'd been
treated by a doctor, and now his body simply had to recover by itself.

If he had the time for that.

The Administrator was livid, and he wasn't a very
calm man at the best of times. Jame was in a holding
cell, instead of in the infirmary, and the Administrator

marched in, his face red, a tic pulsing in one cheek. "Give me back control of the power plant," he demanded.

"Get lost," Jame answered.

The Administrator came over to the bed and let fly with his right hand. The blow slammed into the side of Jame's head. His ears ringing, Jame hardly noticed the extra pain. It took him a minute to recover his wits, though.

"Give me back control," the Administrator repeated.

"So you can kill more people?" Jame asked. "I don't think so."

"You little fool," the man said, his voice cold, low, and furious. "Do you have any idea who you're messing with?"

"The biggest slug in the galaxy?" Jame tensed for another blow, but surprisingly it didn't come.

"The most dangerous man in the solar system," the Administrator informed him. "And you seem to forget that I have hostages. Your father, for example."

Jame's stomach constricted at this threat. He didn't consider himself to be particularly brave, but he would endure what he had to to stop the Administrator. But what if they did something to his father? "I can't give in to you," Jame insisted. "No matter what you do. Because if you get the power back under your control, you'll kill more than my father."

"I'll kill more than him anyway," the Administrator vowed. "I'll kill the both of you in front of the whole city, to set an example."

"Well, you'll never get control back that way," Jame said smugly.

"You don't have control right now," the man pointed out. "So that means somebody else knows the codes you set. At a guess, probably your mother. Do you think *she'll* refuse to give them back to me if the alternative is watching her husband and son die?" He gave a short, barking laugh. "I think not." He spun on his heels, and then said over his shoulder: "Your execution is in one hour. Better get ready for it." He walked out of the cell and sealed it behind him.

One hour to live? Jame huddled in the bed, scared to his bones. He didn't want to die. But, at the same time, he didn't want his mother to give in to the Administrator. The question he wasn't sure about, though, was whether she would feel the same. . . .

Captain Montrose winced as he heard the announcement over the NewsNet. He wasn't at all surprised when Mrs. Wilson came hurrying to see him. They had taken over the substations of the power plant, since they now had the ability to lock out the Administrator's flunkies, and it gave them a good base camp. Despite the losses in the earlier raid, more people were coming over to the rebel cause every hour. Everybody could see what was happening. The Administrator held power for now, but it couldn't last much longer.

Except . . .

"You heard the news?" Mrs. Wilson was distraught. She wasn't carrying her child, Fai; no doubt she'd found someone to look after the little girl, to spare her from hearing the truth. "That man's going to kill my husband and son."

"I heard," Montrose admitted, steeling himself against what he knew was coming.

"We can't let him kill Charle and Jame!" she cried. "We've got to hand the power plant codes to the Administrator!"

"No," Montrose said, as gently as he could. "We can't do that, for two very good reasons."

"We *have* to!" Mrs. Wilson insisted. "I can't let my family die."

"It wouldn't work," Montrose pointed out. "If we handed over the controls again, the Administrator wouldn't let Charle or Jame go — they're too valuable to him as hostages."

"You think he doesn't mean to kill them, then?" she asked, a note of hope in her breaking voice.

Montrose shook his head. "No, I think he *does* mean to kill them. Even though they're more valuable alive, the Administrator is a proud man. He won't let anyone bluff him. If he says they die unless he gets the code, he'll kill them, even if it hurts him."

"And you're just going to *let* him, and say it's all for the good?" Mrs. Wilson asked bitterly. Her eyes were brimming with tears. Montrose realized that the poor woman was totally at the end of her nerves, and could break down at any time. He couldn't blame her, all things considered.

"It's not that bad," he promised her, touching her arm. "I didn't say we'd do *nothing* — just that we couldn't give him what he wanted. I have a better idea. You have control over the power grid right now. The execution is to take place in the main square, so as many people as possible can see it, at six exactly. What I want you to do is to shut down the lighting to the area just before the execution. My forces have infrared helmets, so we'll be able to see perfectly. We'll go in under cover of darkness and get Charle and Jame out without a problem. Then the Administrator won't even have a hostage to hold over our heads."

He saw the hope come back to her eyes. "You really think so?" she asked, her voice shaking.

"I really do. Now get ready for the big moment." He managed a smile. "It's not going to go quite as the Administrator is planning it!"

At a quarter to six, Jame was taken out of his cell by two armed shields. The man and woman both wore armor and face masks; the Administrator was prepared for trouble. Jame only hoped that the man would get it. Outside, in the corridor, he saw his father being taken from the next cell. He looked tired, as if he'd aged a decade while in the cell, but he brightened slightly when he saw Jame. He moved to join him, but his guards held up their tazer rifles, butts ready to hit him.

"You move when we say, and not otherwise," the squad leader said coldly.

His father halted, then called out, "Stay firm, Jame! Don't give in to the creeps!"

The squad leader held up the tazer. "You want to be unconscious for your execution, just keep on disobeying me. Now shut up and come with us. Both of you."

The squad formed around them, and they set off down the corridor toward the main square. The Administrator was making the execution as public as possible. It would serve as a warning to everyone else on Mars of what would happen to anyone causing trouble — or, at least, that was the Administrator's plan. Jame thought it was much more likely to make other people join the revolution, scared that it would be their turn on the execution block next.

His stomach was churning. He was terribly afraid, but he refused to let it show. He wouldn't give these creeps the satisfaction of knowing they'd terrified him. And he had to show the people that somebody could die for his beliefs with dignity. If he could manage it . . .

His father looked tense and tired, but with a kind of inner peace. Jame wished he could share that.

They came out into the main square, and Jame saw that it was about half filled. The Administrator had probably ordered people to attend. Newsbots hovered in the air, covering the event for MarsNet. Jame wondered what the ratings figures for Mars's first ever public execution would be. Maybe he'd die a star. . . . He swallowed, as he saw that there were dozens of other shields in place around the square, covering all approaches. The Administrator probably expected Montrose to attack, and was taking no chances. Shields with tazers were everywhere. How many men did the Administrator have on his side?

Slowly, Jame and his father were led to the center of the square. There was a beautiful fountain there, still running. It was meant to symbolize life on Mars — where there was so little free water — so it seemed ironic that Jame was destined to die in front of it. The guards positioned him and his father, their hands tied behind their backs.

Sweat was trickling down his spine, and he wanted to scream and run for it. He had to force himself not to move. It wouldn't do any good, and he didn't want to go down in history as being shot running away. If he had to die, he'd do it with dignity. His father glanced at him.

"That's my boy," he said proudly. "Don't let them see how scared you are."

"I wish I was braver," Jame whispered back. "Like you."

"Then *I'm* doing a great job of hiding my own fear," his father said. "Believe me, I'm as terrified as you are. But I'll save my last breath to spit in the Administrator's eye."

Jame felt a bit better knowing that his father was scared, too. But it was hard to watch the firing squad moving into position without begging for his life. He didn't want to die. But he had no choice.

His legs felt wobbly as the shields finished getting ready. They stood in a line, their tazer rifles held in front of their chests. A moment later, the Administrator's face appeared on the public screen behind the fountain.

"I am sorry that it has come to this," the Administrator said, trying to sound sincere, but failing miserably.

"But the handful of rebels have left me no option. Wilson and his son are chief among these malcontents, and are sentenced to die. The sentence is to be carried out immediately."

Jame's throat went dry as he heard his death sentence pronounced. *Just a little longer being brave,* he told himself.

The squad leader stepped to one side. "Ready," he called. The six people in the squad brought their weapons up. "Aim . . ." The rifles were raised —

— And all the power went dead in the square. For a second, Jame thought he was dead, because even the sound of the fountain cut off. He couldn't see anything. And then he heard people starting to yell, and realized what had happened.

His mother had taken control and shut down the power!

As quickly as he realized this, he threw himself at where his father had been standing, knocking him to the ground.

Six bolts of electricity crackled through the air where they had both been standing; the squad had fired at where their targets had been. In the blaze of light, Jame saw only shadows and brightness, nothing that made sense. But the men must have realized that they had missed their targets, and would open fire again.

"We've got to move," he gasped, struggling to his feet, which wasn't easy with his hands manacled behind his back. His father was having trouble, too. More flashes of tazer fire lit the darkness, and people were screaming, not knowing what was happening. Jame was astonished when he saw that the bolts weren't coming at him or his father. Then it clicked: Montrose was attacking, and it was *his* troops firing at the would-be executioners!

Jame rose to his feet and stayed by his father. His heart was pounding with excitement and relief. He wasn't dead yet, and maybe he wouldn't be today! He felt someone beside him, a reassuring touch.

"We're with you," the woman whispered. "Hold still; we've infra-sights on. Let us lead you."

"With pleasure," he heard his father say.

A hand took his arm and gently tugged at him. Jame trusted the woman and went along, even though he was completely blind. The woman knew where she was going, avoiding the screaming of the terrified crowd. Some of the shields were trying to fire on the raiders, but they broke off when they couldn't see any targets.

They walked through a door, and into a side corridor. The door hissed closed behind them, and then the lights came on. Jame was blinded for a moment, until his vision adjusted. Then he could see where they were going. The woman leading him was small and stocky, looking odd in the helmet that completely enclosed her head. It had big "eyes" jutting out like an insect, the infra-sights she'd used to lead him this far. Beside them, his father and a young man were moving swiftly. There were no bystanders in the corridor.

"This way," the woman said, taking a second corridor. There were other shields ahead of them, also part of their group, and he could hear steps behind them — the rest of the attackers, obviously. He laughed, joyful to be alive and free again! And with his father. This was too good.

After a few moments, they reached one of the generator substations. "Our base," the woman said, leading them inside. Just inside the door stood Jame's mother, tears of relief streaming down her face. She clutched at him, and then at his father, obviously at a loss for whom to greet first. She couldn't speak, she was so happy. Jame understood perfectly how she felt. He'd never expected to see her again.

The rest of the rebels came in, Captain Montrose last. He had a big grin on his face as he sealed the door behind them. "It's good to see the both of you again," he said by way of greeting.

"You don't know how glad I am to see you," Mr. Wilson said, shaking with relief. "I really thought we were both dead."

"We couldn't let that happen," Montrose said. "Now, let's get those cuffs off you, so you can be normal again." One of his men produced a set of electro-keys, and had the manacles off them both in moments. "There, I'm sure that feels better."

Jame rubbed his wrists. "Definitely," he agreed. "Thank you."

"Glad to help. We couldn't have done it without your program. In fact —"

There was a chime from the far wall, where there was a large Screen. The room was only an entryway to the generator itself, which lay beyond the far wall. This was where the workers normally gathered before they went to their posts, so there was a public Screen. It lit up to show the amused face of the Administrator.

"Montrose. And all the Wilsons! What a surprise. You'll looking rather well, considering you were supposed to be executed."

Jame had a very bad feeling about this; why wasn't the man screaming and cursing? This wasn't like him at all. Unless . . .

"Maybe you could take our place?" Jame's father

suggested. "I'm sure that would be even more popular viewing."

"Oh, very humorous. But you've only delayed matters, I'm afraid, not stopped them." The Administrator smiled. "You see, I *knew* Montrose would attempt a rescue. I had my men all ready for you."

"But they didn't stop us," Montrose objected. He was looking very worried now.

"They weren't meant to stop you, but to track you — which they did." The Administrator looked smug, certain he'd won. "You're surrounded in there now. All of the rebels, I think. Quite a neat way to get you all in one move, don't you think?"

"He's bluffing," Mrs. Wilson said, her face etched with shock. "He can't do anything to us in here. We control the power."

"No," the Administrator said coldly, his good humor evaporated. "You control the generators; I control the *real* power. While we've been talking, my shields have been moving field cannons into place. If you don't surrender and give me the command codes back, they will open fire on you."

"You're insane!" Montrose gasped. "If you fire at us in here, you'll destroy the entire power grid. The city would be without power! Everyone would die."

"Worse than that," the Administrator answered. "I've been told that blowing you up will spread radioactive slag over the entire city. It would poison everyone who might just survive."

"You can't be serious!" Jaime's father said, appalled.

"You don't know me very well, Wilson!" the Administrator roared. "This is *my* world, and I'm not going to be blackmailed by the likes of you! If I can't rule it, then I'll see it dead! And you *know* I'll do it. You have thirty seconds in which to agree to totally surrender, or else my men open fire and everyone dies."

"He's got to be bluffing!" Jame's mother insisted.

"No," Montrose said, his voice sounding like he was being strangled. "He isn't. He'll do it."

"But . . . if we surrender, he wins," Jame said. "We can't give in."

"We have no choice," Montrose said bitterly. "If it was just my life, or even just the few of us here — I'd spit in his face. But if he fires on us here, he'll kill the whole city. And that's unacceptable."

"So we just give in?" asked Jame, hollowly.

"We have to."

Jame's father looked at the screen, where the Administrator was smirking happily, seeing his plan winning. "What assurances do we have that we'll be treated well?" he asked. "I don't ask for me, but for my wife and children."

"You have *no* assurances about *anything*," the Administrator snarled. "You've lost, I've won, and you have to pay the price for your rebellion now. All you can do is surrender or fight. There are no guarantees."

Montrose put his hand on Mr. Wilson's arm. "We have no choice," he said. "We can't let everyone in the city die, no matter what he does to us." He threw down his tazer rifle. "He's won."

Jame stared at the adults in shock as, one by one, they all let their weapons drop.

The unthinkable had happened: The Administrator had won. And not only he and his father were in danger of being killed. So were his mother and Fai.

It couldn't get any worse than this.

"It's all over," the Administrator gloated. "And in plenty of time before Quietus arrives. Mars is ours!"

8

jill Barnes sat behind Peter Chen in the cell on Ice and waited, hardly daring to breathe in case she distracted him. Technically, since he'd been reprieved, he was now her boss once again, but he'd left her in charge of the shields now running the jail. All of the prisoners had recovered and were back in their cells. Barnes had been amazed at how the prisoners were normally treated — the guards simply left them to do as they liked and fend for themselves. This had clearly led to a lot of abuse. Some of the prisoners had been ganging up on others. Marten Scott had managed to run a great deal of Quietus's plans from here without anyone knowing. He had over ten million dollars' worth of computer equipment in his cell!

Barnes had immediately set about reforming the jail. The guards were now down on the prison level, not hidden away up in their sector above. Cells were regularly patrolled. Beatings were stopped, and gangs broken up. And Shimoda had confirmed all of these changes to be permanent. Chen had smiled and approved also, though he insisted this was Barnes's responsibility and not his. He seemed very subdued after his arrest and incarceration. Maybe he'd actually learned something from being on the other side of the law for a change.

But now the jail was in order, and they were awaiting their signal. There was no telling when it would come, and the tension was making everyone nervous. Except, maybe, Chen. He seemed content to sit and wait. He'd hooked in his own Terminal and entered what they'd been able to salvage from Scott's files. The link was there to Quietus, and all that remained was to use it. But first Quietus had to make the call. Surely it wouldn't be much longer? Everything seemed to be moving smoothly toward some culmination of their grand plan. It had to be very soon that they would call for the release of the Doomsday Virus. . . .

Shimoda had called to inform them that Van Dreelen had fled. He was now on Overlook, obviously getting ready for the migration of Quietus to Mars. Shimoda had alerted the shields on the station, and they were — at least theoretically — cooperating fully. Still, to be on the safe side, Shimoda had a backup plan, involving Barnes and the Ramjet now waiting on the runway outside of Ice.

There was a chime, and then the Terminal lit up. Chen and Barnes leaned forward, their nerves strained. Was this it? Luck was on their side, because most of Quietus used fake holo-IDs to disguise their true selves, and Scott — alias the Malefactor — had used a dark, menacing hologram as his contact. The generation program for this had survived the meltdown of his computer, and Chen had it up and running now. The shape of it settled around Chen, following his movements carefully. All the person at the other end of the link would see would be the normal Malefactor image. Barnes stayed out of pickup range. It wouldn't do for her to be seen.

An image formed on the grid, of a tall, silvery humanoid, totally featureless. "Malefactor," the image said, its voice echoing slightly. "This is Rogue."

"Receiving," Chen said, but his voice sounded like the computer-generated one that hid the Malefactor. Secrecy was a wonderful thing!

"Quietus is prepared. You are to unleash the Dooms-day Virus in thirty minutes. You are now recalled to active service. I am downloading the escape codes to your cell. You will be able to walk out of the jail with them. An escape craft will be waiting for you above. Join us on Overlook, berth 247. Do you understand?"

"Perfectly," Chen agreed. "Doomsday Virus is being downloaded . . . now." It looked as though the Malefactor was commencing a program, but Chen had previously set a fake pattern. "The release is irrevocable now."

"Excellent. Don't delay in joining us. If you leave it too late, the virus will isolate you on Earth as well."

"I'll see you soon," Chen answered.

"Quietus appreciates your work, Malefactor," the silver being replied. "And we are now entering our triumph. Rogue out." The silver form vanished as the connection was severed.

"The rats," Chen said softly, severing his side of the connection. The grim Malefactor persona vanished, to be replaced by his scowling face. "Not only are they trying to condemn most of the human race to death, they're even lying to their own man. There's no escape ship waiting for him up top."

"But the escape codes are good," Barnes pointed

out. "Probably they're from Van Dreelen. They wanted Scott to get out of the jail and be stranded in Antarctica."

"By the time he could have made his way back down here, the thirty minutes would have been up," Chen said coldly. "The virus would have been released, and Ice would have been dead."

"Clearing up loose ends," Barnes said furiously. "Killing anyone who knew too much."

"Which means there may be other *loose ends* scheduled to die," Chen pointed out. He sent a signal, and Shimoda's face filled the Screen. "Quietus has sent the message. Thirty minutes to Doomsday."

"Good." Shimoda smiled tightly. "We now know how long we've got. Do you have the escape details?"

"Berth 247 on Overlook," Barnes said. "That's where their ship is waiting."

"Excellent." Shimoda laughed. "We've got them. I'll contact Overlook with the details. Jill — you get moving. Uh . . . Chen . . ." She looked confused. "Technically, I can't give you orders."

Chen nodded. "I know — it's a difficult situation, having two bosses, isn't it? Don't worry, I've volunteered to go along with Lt. Barnes. I'm almost getting used to having her around."

"She does grow on you." Shimoda looked relieved. "Good luck, all of you." She vanished from the Screen.

Barnes gave Chen a quizzical look. "I don't recall hearing you volunteer to help me," she said as he shut everything down.

"You just heard me," Chen answered. As they left the cell, he locked it. They didn't want any other prisoners getting access to this equipment. It would be removed as soon as possible. They moved swiftly through the jail. "Two bosses in one spot is very counterproductive. Shimoda is doing a fine job at Computer Central — perhaps even better than I could, to tell you the truth. She doesn't need me there, interfering with her." He grinned. "But since I outrank you, you're stuck with me here, interfering with you."

"Lucky me," Barnes muttered. Then, remembering he was her boss again, she hastily added, "Sir."

"Don't worry, I won't get in the way," he promised her. "Unless you mess up; then I'm taking over. Until then, look at me as an extra pair of hands." They were now heading up the elevator shaft to the entrance of Ice.

Barnes tapped her wrist-comp. "Pilot, get the Ramjet ready. I'm coming aboard. Make sure the squad is awake and alert, too. Chief Chen will be accompanying us, and I'd hate him to think we're a lazy bunch of layabouts."

The trip out from the guard post to the waiting Ramjet was terrible. The wind had died down at last, and the snow wasn't being blown all over them, but the temperature was still incredibly cold, and even the transport felt to Barnes like she was riding inside a very cold Quikfreez. Thankfully, they reached the Ramjet, and she hurried inside. Out of the Antarctic chill, she could open her jacket again.

"Let's get moving," she ordered as she strapped herself into the closest available seat. Chen took one a few seats ahead of her. The rest of the cabin held her specially picked twenty-person squad. All were armed and looked very alert.

"Takeoff," the pilot called back from his cabin, without any preamble. "Anyone not strapped in, say hello to broken bones."

He wasn't kidding. The ship's engine whined, kicked in, and shot the Ramjet down the short runway, and then screaming into the air. The acceleration pressed Barnes back into her seat, and tore at her body. For a few seconds, it felt like she'd been slapped in the body with a pail of concrete. Then the pressure eased off slightly. There were no windows in the passenger cabin — they had been deemed unnecessary, since this was a shield ship and not a tourist vessel — so she couldn't see out. But they had to be rising at a tremendous speed. The Ramjet kicked in, propelling them even faster.

"Rendezvous with Overlook in forty minutes," the pilot called back. "Last chance to catch some z's, guys."

If only . . . But there was too much to do. As soon as they left gravity behind, the shields could free themselves and spend the time getting their equipment ready. The Overlook shields would raid the ship in berth 247 from inside — and she and her crew would hit it from the outside. Between the two attacks, Quietus would be stopped, finally.

Just a short while now . . .

9

Shimoda strode down the hallway to the meeting room, her mind swirling. She felt elation that this was now all coming to a head. And she felt dread, in case there was something she had missed.

It seemed to be perfect, but she wasn't a fool. There was always something unexpected. What happened then would depend on whether the people she trusted could move fast enough and think on their feet. She'd done all she could to plan for this final battle. The future of mankind was about to be played out, and this was one fight she *had* to win.

The meeting room was ready. She was the first one

there, as she had planned. She took her position and keyed in her codes to the desk-comp there. Tamra's face looked back out at her.

"I'm ready, boss," she promised. "I've tapped into the other comps. I should know within five minutes which of them are real, which are calling in from offices and homes, and which are in space. I'll signal you as soon as I know."

"Good." Shimoda wished she didn't sound so curt, but her nerves were so tense she couldn't help it. If anything went wrong now . . . There had to be some of those shields loyal to Quietus still around. They wouldn't know that they'd been betrayed, and that they'd been left to die. If they got in the way, things could get messy. But she needed to have some shields close by, and had a squad hidden and ready on call. Not everyone who physically attended this meeting might go along with what she had planned, and she needed to have leverage.

The moment of truth was upon them. In a few minutes, she'd *know* who the traitors were — and so would everyone else. And then they could be captured and jailed.

If everything went all right.

There was a chime from her comp, which she answered. The face of the shield commander on Overlook nodded at her. "I've checked the docking records," he said. "The *Miranda* is berthed in 247. Records show she's due to leave in ten minutes. My men have her surrounded, and we'll attack as soon as your ship arrives."

"That will be another fourteen minutes," Shimoda answered. "Can you stall the *Miranda* until then?"

"Oh yes. Trust me, we're really good at technical delays. I'll report back as soon as the raid is over."

"Thank you." She clicked off the connection. It wouldn't do for any Quietus operative to arrive while she was organizing their arrest. Fourteen minutes to go . . .

Van Dreelen was the first to "arrive." He walked into the room, apparently quite real, but Shimoda knew this wasn't the case. "Ah, Taki," he murmured. "Ever the efficient one. Have you decided where you'd like to go for our dinner date?"

What a sick case, she thought. He was still acting as though there were nothing wrong. "I don't recall agreeing to one yet," she said, striving to sound normal. "I'm rather busy right now."

"I'm sure you are," he agreed, taking his seat. "We all are, I think. But I believe in long-range planning. You pick the spot, and I'll pick up the tab."

"I'll get back to you on that one," she promised. *When you're on Ice, where you belong . . .*

One by one, the other board members arrived. Shimoda watched them all come in. It was impossible to tell which ones were real and which were holograms. Oh, she could throw things at them, of course, and the ones that didn't yell "ouch" would be projections. But they could simply be in their offices and unwilling to attend physically, even despite her urging. She had to know which ones were in orbit.

Luther Schein sat down. The Head of Consumer Relations looked bored, but it could just be an act. Anita Horesh of Development took her seat beside him, and they chatted in low voices. Dennis Borden walked in, scowling. The old man was looking frail, but he was one of the senior vice presidents, so he took his seat at the head of the table. Shimoda still didn't know which side the man was on, or if he knew he'd been cloned.

Miriam Rodriguez of Programming moved to sit down, and Badni Jada of Personnel joined her. Anna Fried took her place, still playing with that stylus of hers. Vladek Cominsky of Planning and Ben Quan of Finance arrived together, chattering away. Therese Copin, Head of Technology, arrived alone, nodded at the others, and sat in silence. She looked impatient, as if she had better things to do.

Like running away to Mars?

Finally, Elinor Morgenstein, the president, arrived and

took her seat. She cleared her throat and tapped lightly on the table. "Gentlemen and ladies, this meeting is called to order. Commence recording." She waited for the comp to confirm that the record was being kept, and then she looked at Shimoda. "Miss Shimoda, you called this meeting rather urgently, refusing to explain your reasons until we convened. I think you'd better tell us what is happening now."

Shimoda stood up. Her knees felt weak, but she steeled her nerves. Just a few more minutes, and it would all be over . . . But she had to keep everyone present until then, to be sure. "I must apologize if I over-stepped the limits of my authority," she said meekly. "I know I'm still new to this business, and have a lot to learn. But this meeting truly is very important." She paused for a moment. "We have now uncovered a great deal about our main enemy, Quietus. What I know calls for swift action, which I could not take without the approval of this board." It was amazing how easy it seemed to be to lie like this, since she *had* taken action without their approval. But the best way to keep them occupied was to force them to debate matters. "I hope that you will all agree to back my plans, so that we can capture everyone involved in this conspiracy against the people of Earth."

"Get on with it, woman," Borden groused. "I'm an old

man, and would like to survive this meeting, if possible. What are you blathering on about?"

"Quietus still has access to the Doomsday Virus," she lied again. "I had thought it was destroyed, but one of their members, known as the Malefactor, has a copy of it. We have identified one member of Quietus, a person known as the Controller. She turned out to be Judge Montoya, who is now on Ice. I have ordered her to be given Truzac, to discover how much she can tell us about Quietus. She already revealed the news about the virus. We must identify and stop the Malefactor immediately, before he can release the virus."

"That sounds perfectly reasonable," Van Dreelen said. "And you certainly don't need our authorization to do that. You have that power already."

"I know," Shimoda agreed. *Come on, Tamra.....* "And I've given the order for her to be interrogated. But I know now that she is going to reveal the names of some members of this board itself."

"What?" Copin glared at Shimoda. "You think that Quietus has people on Computer Control itself?"

"No," Shimoda answered. "I *know* they do. The only problem has been identifying them."

"*Has been?*" Van Dreelen asked, sharply. "Does that mean that you have a method of identifying them now?"

"The most obvious one," Shimoda replied. She

tapped her comp. "Lieutenant, bring in your squad, please."

The door opened, and the six shields marched into the room. Each had their tazers at ease, and one carried a box. Shimoda gestured to the box. "If you recall, I did stress the need for you all to be here in person. I am going to give you all Truzac and ask you to state your loyalties."

That was a bombshell, all right! Everyone started talking at once, except those who began yelling. President Morgenstein had to hammer for quiet and raise her voice to get them all settled down.

The president glowered at Shimoda. "You have certainly exceeded the limits of your authority with this move," she snapped. "I'm sure I'm not the only one who is going to demand that you be fired for this."

I'm in real trouble now. Shimoda braced herself and shook her head. The president had no way of knowing that this was all a bluff, of course. Shimoda had no intention of using Truzac. She knew that these proud, sometimes arrogant individuals would never freely submit to such questioning. But if they *believed* she meant to do it, then it would buy her time while they yelled and threatened her. "You have no option," she said, trying to sound as menacing and cold as she could. "These shield operatives are loyal to me and to Computer Control. They will obey my orders and question you all. Anyone who fails is to be arrested. It's that simple."

"You're the one who's simple!" Jada howled, jumping to his feet. "I will *never* agree to such an indignity, and you have no power to force me to do so." He whirled on the shields, who — as she had ordered — were simply standing impassively, supposedly waiting for orders. In fact, they had been strictly instructed not to touch anyone in the room unless Shimoda gave them a direct command.

"We are at war," Shimoda said. "In this event, I think a little loss of dignity is fine, don't you? We have to find out who the traitors in our midst are, or else we're crippled in this battle. I don't care if what I'm doing is legal or not, or if it offends your dignity. Tough. You're going to have to do it."

"She's right," Anita Horesh said abruptly. "We can't fight a war for the future of the human race if we're hampered by not knowing who our foes are. I volunteer to take the Truzac and prove my own loyalty. Are the rest of you going to agree to do likewise? Or must we suspect you all of being traitors?"

"It's not that simple," Morgenstein snapped. "You cannot ask the most powerful people in the world to take a loyalty test and suffer the indignity of a fate associated with criminals."

"Some of us, it seems, *are* criminals," Van Dreelen observed. He seemed to be rather amused by everything that was happening. Well, he could afford to be, since there was apparently no way of touching him. *He* couldn't be given Truzac.

"But that's no reason to accuse *everyone*," spluttered Borden, his face red with anger. "I will not agree —"

Shimoda's comp sounded twice, and Tamra's face materialized. "It's all right, everyone," Shimoda said loudly. "I have no intention of giving anyone Truzac. That was simply a bluff, to earn me some time. And I no longer have any need to uncover the traitors. My secretary has done it for me. Tamra?" She tapped a control, and a hologram of Tamra appeared beside her. Tamra smiled and moved slightly. Everyone's eyes were focused upon her.

"Miss Shimoda didn't tell you everything that we know," Tamra explained. "We know that Quietus has *already* sent the signal to the Malefactor to release the Doomsday Virus."

That caused further consternation, which Shimoda cut off abruptly. "The Doomsday Virus has been destroyed," she announced. "It cannot be released. And Marten Scott, alias the Malefactor, has been neutralized." She couldn't say he was in jail, since she actually had no idea where he was. "Quietus has been defeated, but they didn't know that until this moment. They ordered a retreat from Earth, expecting EarthNet to collapse, and the human race to pretty much die out in the next few months. They were aiming to go to Mars, to take command there and restart their version of the human race. Only it won't be happening. Tamra, which members of the board are projecting here from Overlook?"

"Anna Fried." The woman dropped her stylus, shocked at being identified. It bounced once and vanished from view. "Ben Quan. Vladek Cominsky. Martin Van Dreelen. And, last but far from least, Elinor Morgenstein."

The *president* herself? Even Shimoda was stunned.

"Therese Copin is a hologram," Tamra added, "but she's projecting from her office. I think she's just plain too lazy to walk down there and join you in person."

"So now we know," Shimoda said, grimly. "You four are Quietus traitors, and I'm ordering your arrest immediately."

Morgenstein was no fool. "What lies are these?" she demanded. "This is some kind of power play, isn't it? You're just trying to seize power yourself! *You're* the Quietus agent, trying to muddy the waters and take control by framing us!"

111

"It's no use," Shimoda countered. "If you're not on Overlook, simply prove it." She threw her stylus onto the table. "Pick that up!"

"I'm not playing games with you!" the president snarled. She looked at the shields. "Arrest her, immediately! I am the president, and I order it!"

That was a blow Shimoda hadn't expected. Technically, the woman *was* in charge, even if the shields were loyal to Computer Control, and not to Quietus. The lieutenant hesitated, wondering who to obey. Shimoda knew that things would get messy in moments if she didn't take command. She moved quickly, leaping onto the conference table, and threw herself at the president's seat. There was a shocked gasp, and several people moved, including the shields, but none in time.

Shimoda went right through the hologram of Morgenstein — and hit the empty chair. "Ouch," she complained, as she bruised her shoulder and then fell to the floor. She staggered back to her feet, brushing her hair from her eyes. "She's not here," she said, triumphantly. "Are you?"

Morgenstein's image stood looking at her, and then it abruptly cut out. So did Van Dreelen's, Quan's, Fried's, and Cominsky's. The people left in the room looked completely stunned. Before anyone could start howling, complaining, or questioning, Shimoda took command.

"The traitors have been uncovered," she said. "And even as we speak, I have an operation under way to capture them and bring them back to Earth for trial. They will not escape us. Meanwhile, we have to work swiftly." She looked around the table. "Mr. Borden, you are the senior member here now. I believe the presidency falls to you?" So he *hadn't* known about his clone, after all. He was going to get a surprise when she brought him up to date!

Bemused, the old man blinked, and then nodded. "Yes, young lady, I do believe you are quite correct. Though it is a trifle irregular, I think we can take it that Miss Morgenstein, Miss Fried, Mr. Cominsky, and Mr. Van Dreelen have effectively handed in their resignations. You do seem to have matters in hand, though, so perhaps you can finish illuminating those of us who are left?" He glanced at Copin. "And maybe you could do as you're told for once, and get your backside down here!" The woman blushed, and then her image vanished. She was clearly hurrying down in person.

"Quietus is on Overlook," Shimoda explained. "They are planning to flee to Mars on a ship called the *Miranda*. I have two forces of shields converging on it at this moment. They will arrest everyone aboard, and they will be transported back to Earth to stand trial. Under Truzac questioning, we'll get to the end of this bunch of traitors very shortly."

"Excellent." Borden looked rather pleased. "Young lady, your methods may be . . . shall we say *unorthodox*? But they do appear to be very effective. I think I speak for everyone when I say that the board will back you in whatever you feel must be done. At least, I *trust* I speak for everyone?" There was a hasty nodding all around the table. The board members looked relieved that they had come through all this unscathed. The door opened, and Therese Copin came in, bright red, and slipped quietly into her seat — for real this time.

"Good." Borden looked over to Shimoda. "Now what?"

"There does seem to be one last problem associated with Quietus that we need to address," she said. "They have been using illegal cloning technology, which we have to trace and stop. And there is one member of Quietus I do not believe will be with the others. His name is Devon, and he's the creator of the Doomsday Virus."

Rodriguez looked puzzled. "I thought you had captured the person who created the virus," she objected.

"So did I," admitted Shimoda. "But I was wrong. Tristan Conner is innocent, and he must be pardoned by the board. Devon is his clone."

"Understood," Borden said. He glanced around the room. "I think it is clear that Miss Shimoda is doing an excellent job. I see no reason why she should not have the authority to pursue this Devon. Any objections?" There were none. "Well, I think we've got a lot to think about now," he said. "We need to find replacements for our . . . missing board members. That will take some pondering, I'm sure. Meanwhile —"

Shimoda's comp chimed again. That had to be Jill Barnes. Shimoda felt a great sense of relief, knowing that everything was over. They had identified and captured Quietus, and everything was finally winding down nicely. "Excuse me." She tapped to receive the transmission.

It was Barnes, but she didn't look happy. Shimoda's stomach lurched. "Sorry, chief," Barnes reported. "We've run into problems. Berth 247 contains the *Miranda*, all right — but it's completely empty. There's nobody aboard it. It was a diversion. The members of Quietus must have boarded a different ship. They've escaped."

Shimoda felt sick. Despite everything, she'd been outsmarted at the end. Quietus was still free — and who knew what they would do next?

10

Tristan realized that the old saying was definitely true: You could have too much of a good thing. Genia claimed she wasn't interested romantically in Tristan, but she was certainly acting pretty jealous of his attention. And Mora claimed she was just along because she felt guilty for how she'd let Tristan down, and now wanted to make it up to him. Tristan was afraid he'd literally have to break up a fight soon.

"I don't understand why we can't just take a regular flight up to the space station," Mora complained, as they looked out over the launch field at Schwarzenegger

Spaceport in Newark. "There are plenty of them still going up."

"You don't understand much of *anything*," Genia complained. "Listen, thick-as-a-brick, Tristan's on the Most Wanted list. And he's already taken a space plane up. He'd never get away with doing the same trick twice. The shields have got to be looking at all outgoing flights for him."

Mora glared at the other girl. "Can't he wear a disguise or something?"

Genia rolled her eyes. "He can't disguise his DNA, you jerk. And we need a sample to get a ticket."

"Calm down," Tristan said, hoping to chill them both out. "There are two other reasons why we can't use a regular shuttle. First, we're going to the Moon and not Overlook. A commercial flight stops at Overlook, true, and changes. That's twice through security, and even if we got away with it once, we'd never manage it twice. The second reason is that Devon's a devious character, and he might realize we're on his trail. I don't *think* he knows, but I'm not going to rely on that. So if he sees us coming, I'm sure he'll try to kill us. If he does, I'd like to have the chance to change our plans. Besides, on a passenger ship, there would be lots of others people whose lives would be placed in jeopardy if we were with them."

"So we're going in a garbage barge?" Mora asked, wrinkling her nose. "Excuse me for not applauding the idea."

"It's not a garbage barge." It was getting harder and harder to keep his temper with her lousy attitude. He was starting to wonder what he'd ever seen in her anyway. Aside from her great figure and gorgeous face, of course. "It's a recovery ship. The crew areas will be very pleasant, I promise. There are only two real crew members along. I've faked us IDs as reporters. We're doing a story for a college Web site about junk recovery from the Moon. These guys will be happy to see their names on the Net, so they'll be real nice to us."

"Whatever you call it, they still deal in trash," Mora said. She sighed. "Not too romantic."

Genia glared at her. "Excuse me? Can't you make up your mind whether you want Tristan, or want him dead?"

Mora glared back. "I've resigned myself to the knowledge that my behavior has lost his affections. But I still have feelings for him."

"Feelings?" Genia was simmering. "Maybe you should . . . scratch them? Or I'd be happy to do it for you." She showed her nails.

"Girls!" Tristan said unwisely. "Don't fight over me."

Genia sniffed loudly, and threw her head back.

"We're not fighting over *you*. We're just fighting." She gave him a stare that chilled him to his toes. "And as I keep saying, you're *way* too young for me."

"You keep *saying* it," Mora objected. "But I don't see you bowing out of this trip. After all, the shields aren't hunting you any longer. You could go home again."

"To the Underworld? I seem to recall you trashed my place, which is something else I owe you for."

Tristan decided his best bet was to ignore them. It was quite clear that nothing he could do or say would change anything — except to get them annoyed. He hoped he could ignore the distraction of their constant fighting. He concentrated on finishing off his fake credentials and back story. He was *fairly* sure the shields couldn't check every ship leaving Earth, and this garbage barge was his best bet. Ships like this never carried passengers, so what would there be for the shields to check?

That was the idea, at least.

"We're done," he told the girls, interrupting them midargument. "I suggest we get aboard."

"Down time!" Genia said scornfully. "Look, it may be a matter of male pride to wear the same clothes two weeks running, but I for one want some new stuff."

"You do indeed," Mora agreed, with mock sweetness. "You're starting to smell."

"Take a whiff of your own air before you criticize me," Genia growled.

"We'll get some new clothes," Tristan said hastily. He was glad that Genia still had her implant-copying device on her. He didn't approve of her stealing from her victims, but right now they had very little choice in the matter. None of the three of them had their own working ICs any longer. Genia had never had one; he'd destroyed his own to cover his tracks; and Mora's had been disconnected when she was sent on Ice. The only good part of all of this was the fact that the shields could no longer track their movement. If Genia hadn't been able to copy chip data from people she passed by, they'd be in deep trouble. "I'll even get some new clothes, too. It would look suspicious if we went aboard the ship without some belongings."

Shopping shut the two girls up, at least. One of the nice things about spaceports was that they had real shops in them, so people could buy presents and take them on their flights. It was far more convenient than shopping in a virtual mall and trying to get stuff delivered. Takeout to a spaceport would have looked very suspicious. The girls bought extra clothing and accessories, along with bags to carry them in. He bought a bag of his own and a change of clothes. No matter how well clothing was made, even in this day and age it started getting stinky after a week. He wished he had time for a shower, but that should be possible on the ship. Flight time to the Moon was twelve hours, and the craft did have complete crew facilities.

When they were ready, it was only twenty minutes till liftoff. The captain of the garbage barge was expecting them, and the fake IC Genia was using was programmed to get them past the checkpoints to the crew section of the port. Tristan felt a twinge of envy as they passed the regular passengers getting ready for one of the more luxurious ships to space.

They passed down several corridors, and through three "Employee Only" doors before they reached the gate holding their ship, the *Simón Bolívar*. They punched in, and the hatch opened for them. "That you, guys?" asked a woman's voice from a speaker by the hatch.

"It's us," Genia confirmed, since she was supposed to be in charge of the interviews. "Can we come aboard now?"

"Come on up," the woman answered. "Straight ahead, down the corridor to the elevator. Take it right to the bridge. And don't hang around — I'd like to have you strapped in before we lift off, but I'm going up in ten minutes, whether you're ready or not."

"Got that," Genia confirmed. "Let's go, guys."

Tristan looked around as they made their way to the elevator. The ship was dirty, mostly solid walls and struts. There was no attempt to pretty the place up, unless you counted the graffiti on the walls. After reading a couple, Tristan decided that it wasn't there for art's sake, but to let off steam.

"It's filthier than I imagined," Mora muttered. "Thanks a lot, Tristan."

"You can always get off," Genia suggested.

"No thanks. If you can slum it, so can I."

"Look on the bright side," Genia said, smiling cheerfully. "It's still better than living in the Underworld and wearing a blanket, isn't it?"

"Girls!" Tristan said warningly.

"Shut up!" they both said at the same moment. Tristan shut up.

The bridge wasn't a whole lot better. It was cleaner, at least, but it was also obviously both old and well-worn. The seats were serviceable but battered. The panels looked as if they had been built a century ago. Tristan didn't want to know how old their onboard computer was, or how slow. He suspected the desk-comp he had in his pack had more memory and speed than the one powering this ship.

There were two people in their seats already, obviously the crew. They sat amidst all of the equipment, going through a checklist, ready for launch. One was an aging man, going bald on the top of his head and looking kind of tired. He was the first mate, Brightman. The captain was a little younger, though no longer young, and her blond hair was shot through with gray streaks. She concentrated on her tasks at hand, and waved vaguely at the four extra seats at the back of the room. "Sit down, belt up, and be quiet," she said by way of greeting. "Record what you like, but don't bother us till we're clear of Earth and I talk to you first."

Tristan meekly did as he was told. Mora pointedly strapped herself in beside him. Just as deliberately, Genia left a gap between herself and Mora. Then she took out her vid recorder and set it working, to keep up their cover story. Tristan wondered if his nerves would stand up to this, but he pushed his own feelings into the background.

They now knew where Devon was. Once they were on the Moon, Tristan was certain he'd be able to track down his clone. Then would come the showdown. If only he could be as certain that he would beat Devon as he tried to sound. Even with Genia and Mora to help, he felt inadequate. Devon was very devious and aggressive. And he didn't have the scruples that Tristan was working with; Devon would do *anything* to win.

Tristan wondered how much of a chance he stood.

And his mind kept coming back to that one, terrible fact: Both of his clones were criminals. . . . So far, he'd been able to do what he knew was right, whatever the cost. But would he be able to keep that up? Or was he genetically destined to become a criminal too?

"Here we go," Captain O'Connell announced, and the ship's engines roared to life. The acceleration thrust him back into his seat as the *Simón Bolívar* lifted from its cradle and roared upward toward the waiting stars.

11

Shimoda's hands were shaking, and she had to clasp them in her lap so that nobody else would see. She closed her eyes for a second and took a deep breath, trying to compose herself. Then she stared at the image of Lieutenant Barnes. "Jill," she asked, "how did we lose them?'

"They had a second ship prepared," Barnes answered sourly. "While we were concentrating on the *Miranda*, they were embarking on this other ship and getting under way. They *knew* we were after them."

"I don't think so," Chen cut in. "I think they're just naturally paranoid, and had a second ship prepared anyway. This wasn't a last-minute decision." He looked worried. "According to the official logs, no ships have left Overlook in the past two hours, but eight have arrived. And Morgenstein was on one of those eight."

"So," Borden said, coming up behind Shimoda, "you're saying they're still aboard Overlook?"

"No," Chen answered. "I'm saying they want us to *think* that. They may have lost their computer genius, Devon, but Cominsky is quite a brilliant programmer. He has to be, as Head of Planning. I think the records have been doctored, and that a ship *has* left the station on its way to Mars. They're trying to delay us looking for them."

"Can't you just pick them up on radar?" Luther Schein asked.

"If we could, we would have," Chen snapped, obviously getting annoyed. "There's a bug in the radar system. It's working fine for close in to the station, but out more than five miles, it's getting nothing. There are repair people working on it, but they're not optimistic about an early fix. Quietus has planned this well. They're on their way to Mars, and we don't know precisely where they are, nor do we know what ship they're in." He wiped his brow. "Look, I'll do what I can here, and call you back as soon as we have any news. But I'm not particularly optimistic right now. Chen out." The link died.

Shimoda sat back in her chair, worried sick. After all this, to lose Quietus now! There had to be *something* they could do. The trouble was, her mind was coming up blank. "I'm open to suggestions," she admitted wearily.

"We know they're going to Mars," Jada said. "Can't we just get the Martian shields to arrest them?"

"You haven't been paying attention," Shimoda informed him. "The shields on Mars are loyal to Quietus. We're not getting much information out of there, but it looks like the Administrator is a high-up in Quietus, and he's taken over control of the seven cities of Mars, using his shield thugs. Technically, by interplanetary law, we're not allowed to intervene in an internal problem on Mars. Practically, I'd say let's forget the law and work on getting some shock troops up there to free Mars again."

"It's not that simple," Borden said. He, too, sounded very weary. Sometimes Shimoda forgot he was in his nineties; he looked twenty years older than that right now. "The Administrator has contacted me privately. I was going to share this with the rest of you later, but — well, it seems appropriate now." He moved back to his seat and tapped controls on his hand-comp.

The image of the Martian Administrator formed, along with a date and time stamp. "Borden, I'm telling you this once, and expect you to pass it on to the rest of the Board. I have control on Mars, and I'm not giving it up again. I have all the power plants mined, and I alone have the triggering key. If Earth tries to interfere, I will detonate all of the explosives. Mars will lose power, and that means everyone here will die in a couple of hours."

"You wouldn't be that insane!" Borden's voice replied.

The Administrator smiled tightly. "I've put my life, my career, and my dreams on the line here, Borden. If I go down, I'm taking Mars with me. This is not open to negotiation." The image died.

Borden looked around the room. "I don't think we can afford to try an assault on Mars. I'm absolutely certain he isn't bluffing. If we try and dethrone him, he'll kill every man, woman, and child there."

Shimoda hadn't thought she could feel any sicker, but she discovered that she'd been wrong. This was getting worse and worse. "Then we have to stop Quietus before they reach Mars," she said slowly. "Once they get there, they'll be untouchable."

"Forget Quietus for a second," Copin said. "I have family on Mars. My sister and her kids. The Administrator is holding them all hostage. We have to do something to help them, too."

"What *can* we do?" Shimoda asked bitterly. "We can't send in troops."

"Maybe a special agent? Or a team?" Anita Horesh suggested. "We have to have some kind of strike force that could do the job."

"Probably," Shimoda agreed. "But don't you think the Administrator will be expecting that? Don't forget, four members of this board are on their way to join him. I'm sure they've betrayed most of our secrets to him by now. We have to start over again and build from the beginning. It's the only way we can get around the loss of security. *Then* we can strike."

"And how long will that take?" asked Copin. "How long must my sister and her family suffer? And all the others caught in Quietus's web?"

"I don't know!" Shimoda yelled. "I'm just a shield, who's *way* out of her depth here! I haven't been trained for any of this. I'm making it all up as I go along. I know you're expecting miracles from me, but don't expect them immediately, okay?"

That burst of temper subdued everyone for a moment. Then Borden nodded. "You're right, my dear —

we're expecting too much, too soon. You need time to think and plan." He looked pointedly at Therese Copin. "And some of us are not helping with our attitudes. I think we should recess this meeting and *all* consider possibilities and options. Nobody leave the building, and everyone be ready to meet again at any moment. We can't rest until this is all settled."

Everyone, subdued, agreed with this plan. One by one, they all filed out of the room, heading for their own offices. Only Borden remained behind for a moment with Shimoda. He moved over and rested a hand on her shoulder. "You're wrong, you know."

Shimoda laughed bitterly. "Yes, I've been wrong about a lot of things, haven't I? You should fire me, you know, and put Chen back in charge."

"Chen's in space." Borden shook his head. "Besides, you've done everything you could. More than everything, in fact. I'm amazed at what you've accomplished, despite the work of those traitors. Anyway, what you're most wrong about is being nothing but a shield. You're a very tough, very imaginative young lady. I have every confidence in you."

"Well, that makes one of us."

"You're tired," Borden told her. "Understandably. Go and get some rest, drink some coffee, and scream at your secretary. Whatever makes you feel better. Then

I'm sure you'll get back on the case and figure out what we can do."

Shimoda stood up, sighing. "I hope you're right," she said. "Because at the moment, everything's totally messed up. We've lost Mars, we've lost Quietus, we've lost Devon, we've lost Connor and Genia. . . ." Her voice trailed off.

"But we've regained Computer Control," Borden pointed out. "And we've destroyed the Doomsday Virus, so EarthNet is safe. The human race isn't going to die today. I think that's not a bad success rate for one day." He managed a weak smile. "Haven't you ever seen *Gone With the Wind*?" he asked her. "Tomorrow's another day, you know. Fight tomorrow's battles then. Today, just get some rest."

Rest? Shimoda moved away from the table obediently. But with everything still hanging over her head, she didn't see how she could ever rest again.

12

Devon sat back in the pilot's chair of the shield commander's ship. It was really a fine little vessel. Perfect for one person, but roomy enough for a family — if he happened to have one. The vessel was long, slender, and rather sleek. The control room was at the apex, and that was where he was seated. Aft of this was the general room, then the galley and four private rooms, nicely furnished. Devon had slung his few possessions down on the bed in the largest one, then headed to the control room. It had taken him a very short while to discover he'd have absolutely no problem flying the ship.

It wasn't that he was a skilled pilot — he'd never flown a ship before, in fact. But there was a really smart interface comp aboard that ran things. All he had to do was to tell it where he wanted to go, and how fast, and then let it do the work. Right now, he was getting the ship fueled up. While he was waiting, he fixed himself some food in the galley.

This was the life! If only he could live in this ship always. The commander had very rich tastes, and the small lockers were stocked with rare caviar, lots of smoked salmon, and plenty of snack foods. He fixed himself some hot peanut nukes, and munched as he checked out the rest of the ship. It was almost a shame he didn't have any friends — he could throw a terrific party here! Lots of entertainment discs, tons of food, and a music system to die for.

But if he was going to become master of Earth, he'd have to live there. He could always get them to build him some sort of palace where he could throw parties. There would be plenty of people who'd want to get to know him once he was in charge, and they'd party if he ordered it.

Munching away, he finished touring the ship. Nice, very nice indeed. He'd be happy here the couple of days he needed it. Maybe he'd keep it as a space yacht. Or maybe he'd get himself something better.

He returned to the control room to see that the fueling was finished. Excellent. Putting the nuts down, he strapped himself into the pilot's seat, and then donned the helmet that enabled him to interface with the controlling computer. It enveloped his head and projected a realistic view of what was outside the ship, as if he were the ship itself.

"Prepare for launch," he ordered.

"We have not received clearance," the computer reminded him. It had a pleasant female voice, obviously the one programmed by the shield commander.

"We don't need clearance," Devon answered. "We go when I feel like it."

"We do need clearance," the computer argued. "Otherwise I cannot launch."

Pushy computer intelligences . . . Devon considered giving this one a personality wipe, but that would affect its operation. Instead, he hooked into the main computers, registered a flight plan, and gained approval. As soon as the code was transmitted, he wiped his plans. He didn't want anybody knowing what was happening — they might warn Earth. Now that the ship had clearance, its computer was happy, and set about doing prelaunch checks. While it did so, Devon started work on the rest of his sabotage.

First of all, he hijacked the command codes for the

nuclear generators, and then switched to his own comps. Once they were in control, he started their countdown. In twelve hours, they'd all blow, and it was *bye-bye, Moon*. That would be fun. But not fun enough.

"One minute to launch," the computer informed him.

"Fine, just do it, okay?" He was absorbed in his work. He hacked into the controls for the docking bay, and overrode the loading crane commands. As soon as his ship lifted off, the crane would malfunction and slam through the airlock door so it wouldn't close again. That would leave the bay needing repair work — about a day of it.

The ship shuddered as the power plant kicked in, and then it kicked again as the ship lifted off. It was a wild ride. He was still in VR, so he got the full effect of it. The docking bay's roof was open, and the ship rose up and out of it. The bleak, serene landscape came into view, all dust-gray as far as the eye could see. Craters piled on craters, stretching to the horizon. Very little of Armstrong City was visible from the surface — just the six docking port airlocks, the other five all closed right now, and some access areas. The city itself was constructed below the ground. This was so lunar dust and rocks could protect the city against meteorite strikes and the radiation from solar flares.

The humans on the Moon lived in high-tech burrows. And soon they'd die there, trapped and helpless.

Devon switched the view from ahead to behind. He could see past the exhaust to the airlock from which his ship had just launched. The huge doors started to close again, so the port could be readied for its next use. Then the crane swung across, its long arm jutting through the opening. The doors closed on it, and all of them cracked and buckled, leaving a horrible mess.

Alarms rang on Devon's panel, since he was still hacked into the system. Perfect! They wouldn't be using that lock again in a hurry! Now to seal off the others . . . As his ship rose from the Moon, thrusting up into the star-speckled blackness above, Devon set about destroying the other five locks. Three held ships, so he simply caused the fuel loaders to break free. The super-cold fuel, filled with liquid oxygen, spilled down in an arc. Devon caused sparks, and fire howled throughout the three locks. In two of them technicians were enveloped before they could even scream. Three ports became blazing infernos, melting metal and plastic, rendering the locks completely useless.

The other two were currently empty, being prepared to receive incoming ships. Devon opened their airlocks and then rammed the cranes through them, as he'd done with his own port. Wonderful.

Naturally, his presence was detected, as he'd known it would be. He'd made no attempt to hide himself.

After all, where was the fun in doing all of this if nobody knew you were responsible?

An incoming message flashed. Devon came out of VR to answer it, lifting his helmet and then picking up the rest of his peanut nukes to munch as he talked. The face of Moss, the governor's aide, filled the Screen.

"Are you the maniac that the governor's been talking about?" Moss demanded, his face pale with shock.

"I think you could manage something a little more flattering than *maniac* if you tried," Devon answered with a grin. "But other than that, yes, I'd say that sounds like me."

"He really is innocent?"

Devon shrugged. "Well, he's guilty of being an idiot. Other than that, and trying to embezzle about four billion dollars from the general fund . . . yes, I guess he's innocent."

"What have you done to our docking ports?"

This was getting tedious already. Devon was starting to feel bored. "If you check your instruments, you'll see that I've rendered them unusable for at least a day. Maybe longer — those were pretty good fires."

"Why did you do that?" demanded Moss.

"Two reasons," Devon answered around the mouthful of nuts. "First, so you couldn't send any ships after me to bring me back. Second, so you couldn't escape."

Moss was completely confused. "Escape?"

"Don't you *ever* check your instruments?" Devon chided him. "Well, take a look at the reports from the power stations. I'll hold."

Moss vanished from the Screen, and then reappeared a couple of minutes later. Incredibly, he managed to look even paler and more scared than before. "What did you do to the generators?" he gasped.

"Set them to blow," Devon explained, sighing. "As in *boom! you're dead!* In twelve hours, in fact. Oh, don't even bother trying to get control of them back. You'll never dispose of my command codes in so short a time. Just get used to the fact that you're going to all be medium-rare chunks of steak in half a day."

"Why?" Moss howled. "Why are you doing this?"

Devon shrugged. "Why climb a mountain? Why surf the Net, or write a symphony? Because it's there, because you can, because it's a work of art. And besides, you people have irritated and bored me, and I don't like that. It's very rude, and this is my solution to your bad manners. Trust me, the universe is better off without you losers around. So sit back, relax, and have a nice death. I know I'll have fun watching it." He cut the transmission off. The comp chimed again, but he ignored it. He would have sealed off incoming messages, but he might want to see the Lunies all panicking again before they died. That should be a lot of fun.

Well, that was the Moon all fixed. They couldn't possibly do anything to stop what he planned, so he forgot about them for the moment and turned to Earth instead. Time to call home . . .

First he checked on the freighter he'd fixed up. It had launched earlier, and was well on the way to Earth by now. It was still firmly under his control. He had already bugged the radar equipment on Overlook and Earth's early warning satellites. Neither would be able to detect the approach of his freighter or his ship, so no bright spark could launch a missile and try to shoot either down. The freighter's Screens came up on his command. It was right on schedule. The computer was driving it just as he'd programmed.

Perfect. Now came the most fun call of all. To Computer Control itself.

It was time to rule the world.

Or destroy it.

13

Shimoda's headache was worse, and no amount of No-pain was helping her. The med-dispense was advising medical treatment but there was no time for gene therapy. She'd been concentrating for several hours, and Tamra had been bringing fresh extra-strength coffee every twenty minutes. Shimoda couldn't remember drinking any, but the old cups were always empty when Tamra took them away.

She'd gotten nowhere at all since the meeting. There had to be a solution to all of this, but she simply couldn't see it. Maybe she was trying too hard, or maybe she'd reached the limits of her meager abilities. She didn't know. But she couldn't figure out how to find Quietus, and she didn't know what to do about Mars.

It really wasn't fair. No matter what Computer Control thought of her, making her Head of Security had been Van Dreelen's whim, and he'd obviously done it because he felt sure she'd mess the job up. And she had. He'd left her in power because he knew she'd never be able to stop Quietus. After all, she was just a shield, really, not a superwoman. She was fine at catching crooks; saving the world was *way* out of her league!

It wasn't fair — but who else could do it? Borden was a nice man, but old and not blessed with great ideas anymore. And the others were mostly bureaucrats, not geniuses.

Speaking of which, she wished that she had Genia here now. Maybe the little thief would have a bright idea. She was very inventive. Or even Connor. That boy had been telling the truth all along, it seemed. And that meant he really *had* worked out how to stop the Doomsday Virus. Perhaps he was just the genius who could work out how to save Earth as well? She sure couldn't.

But she was on her own. Oh, she had access to any brains on Earth that she could find. The trouble was that she didn't know if she could trust them, or even how good they were.

It was all one huge, rotten mess, and it was up to her to somehow save the day.

She gazed out of her window at the Japanese garden. It was supposed to calm her spirit and make her feel more tranquil. Right now, she felt like running out there, grabbing one of the carefully positioned rocks, and heaving it through a window. Breaking glass might calm her nerves a bit. But she couldn't do that. It was against all of her training.

She wished she could just walk out and leave this whole, horrible mess for someone else to deal with. Why should she be stuck with it? It wasn't fair!

The comp chimed, showing an incoming message. "Tamra!" she yelled. "Get that. I don't care if it's Gabriel come to blow his horn and announce Judgment Day — I don't want to be disturbed!"

Tamra's face peeked around the door. "I can't answer it," she said, puzzled. "It's for Computer Control members only. An emergency code I didn't even know existed. It has to be handled by you."

That was weird. And, coming as it did now, scary. It had to be Van Dreelen, or one of the others. Nobody else would know of such a code, would they? She really didn't want to face one of those rats again, but she realized that it had to be very important, so she gestured for Tamra to stay, and then hit the *accept* button.

A very familiar face filled her terminal. "Connor?" she asked. How had *he* found the emergency codes? Stupid question — the kid was a genius hacker!

"Not hardly," the face replied, a quirky grin forming. "My name's Devon."

Devon . . .

"You," she whispered, not knowing whether to be furious or appalled. "This is all your fault!"

"I like to think so, yes," he agreed modestly. "It's one of the burdens of genius — having to take the rap for what you do. So — how's life down there? Still going on?"

"No thanks to you." Shimoda stared at the youth. Now that she knew it was Tristan's clone-twin, she could see very slight differences, mostly in the cocky attitude this kid possessed. Tristan was much less egotistical. "You do know your Doomsday Virus is dead, don't you?"

He shrugged. "Que sera, sera," he quipped. "No big deal. I can live without it. The question at the moment is — can you?"

"What are you talking about?" Shimoda demanded. She had a very bad feeling about all of this.

"You want a sneak preview of my plans?" He shook his head. "No can do. I don't want to have to repeat myself. Just call an emergency meeting of Computer Control, and I'll explain everything, once, to all of you."

"You don't give me orders," Shimoda said stubbornly.

"Then consider it a request — one that will destroy the human race if you refuse, okay? Get with it, lady. I'll call back in five minutes, and you'd better be ready. You don't get any more chances." The image died.

Shimoda groaned. "Tamra, call the meeting. Then come with me. I may need you."

"For support?"

"No, to kill me if things get any worse. And I think they're about to . . ." Wearily, she walked down to the conference room once again and collapsed into her chair. Tamra joined her a moment later, and then, one by one, the other board members filed in and took their seats.

"What's happening?" Miriam Rodriguez asked. She looked terrible, at least as bad as Shimoda had to appear.

"More trouble," Shimoda replied. "Like we needed

it. Devon has reappeared, with his own nasty little plan."

"Just when I thought things couldn't get worse," Luther Schein muttered. He needed to cream his beard away; he looked awful.

Borden was the last in, looking exhausted and double his age. After a moment's hesitation, he took the president's seat. "Let's get on with it," he grumbled. "I don't think my heart can take many more shocks."

"We're just waiting for Devon to call back," Shimoda explained. "He's the young maniac who developed the Doomsday Virus, and framed Tristan Connor for the deed. I gather he's been up to something while we didn't know he existed."

"Terrific," Copin said dully.

The comp chimed, and Tamra tapped to route the call here. A hologram appeared, standing on the table and looking down at them all.

"You're probably wondering why I called this meeting," Devon said, grinning cheerily at them. "Trust me, it's not because I love to see your happy faces. You all look lousy. What's up, some politician stopped your pensions?"

"Get on with it," Schein snarled. "Stop baiting us."

"And miss all of the fun?" Devon shrugged. "Okay,

if you insist, let's cut right to the chase. I want command of the Omega Circuit, and I want it now. Otherwise Earth dies. There, is that direct enough for you?"

Shimoda shook her head. "What are you talking about?" she asked. She was almost beyond shock now. "What's this Omega Circuit?"

Devon glanced at Borden. "Hi. You got a promotion? I thought the witch-woman always sat there."

"The *witch-woman* is a member of Quietus," Borden answered. "And she's on her way to Mars."

"No loss. I hate a person with no sense of humor. Okay, smiley, *you* explain to the novice there what I want."

Borden took a deep breath before looking at Shimoda. "In the heart of Computer Control, the original planners built an override. The Omega Circuit. It's sealed and has never been used. It requires the full approval of all of the board to engage it. Once it is engaged, it takes over Computer Control completely. It's the ultimate line in control — whoever possesses command of the Omega Circuit controls EarthNet — and, though it, Earth."

"Pretty neat explanation," Devon said approvingly. "You just *look* like you're old and boring, then." He winked at Shimoda. "That's it — and what he didn't say is that once the Omega Circuit is engaged, it can't ever be turned off. Only the person who has command of it can use it. If anything happens to that person, EarthNet seizes up and everybody dies. So there we are, that's what I want — access to the Omega Circuit so I can run things. Get the picture?"

"Not quite," Shimoda said slowly. "I know what you *want*. But why should we ever even consider giving you that kind of power? If you get the Omega Circuit control, you'll become the invincible ruler of Earth."

"Yes, well, that *is* kind of the idea," Devon said. "I might keep you around as my court jester. Can you juggle?"

"I can't think of any reason why I'd agree to give you that kind of power," Shimoda answered. Nobody else was talking. Why were they leaving all of this to her?

"Well let's see if I can give you a teeny, weensy one, okay?" He brought up a picture of Earth, spinning between his hands. "This is Earth, right? Well, I've got a freighter heading toward it now, perfectly hidden from detection. Don't even think about trying to find it or shoot it down. Anyway, it's TK-943. Look it up in the records. You'll see that it's carrying depleted radioactive ore. It's supposed to be heading for the heart of the Sun, where it would burn up harmlessly." He grinned. "That is, before I reprogrammed it to head back home. Right now, it's coming toward Earth at full thrust. When it reaches the upper atmosphere, I'll trigger a tiny little bomb in the tummy of the ship. This will spill it open and scatter its contents all over the upper atmosphere. If you've got some spare time, you can check my calculations, but I think I'd be correct in saying that dumping several thousand tons of highly radioactive ores into Earth's biosphere would kill every single living thing on the planet in days. People. Trees. Grass. Bugs. Germs. *Everything*. Get the picture?"

Shimoda did, only too well. If the ore was spilled, the jet stream would carry the dust over the whole planet in a matter of days. It would fall from the sky, gently covering everything on Earth.

And then killing whatever it touched.

Nothing could survive. *Nothing!* Every last living thing on Earth would perish. It was worse than the Doomsday Virus; that would only kill people. *This* would wipe every last vestige of life from the planet.

She wanted to protest that he was lying, that this couldn't be happening. But she could see from looking at him that he was absolutely, utterly deadly serious about this.

What a choice — hand complete control of the

human race over to him — or face the absolute de-
struction of life on Earth . . .

To be concluded in:

2099: Book #6:

firestorm

about the author

JOHN PEEL is the author of numerous best-selling novels for young adults. There are six books in his amazing Diadem series: *Book of Names, Book of Signs, Book of Magic, Book of Thunder, Book of Earth,* and *Book of Nightmares.* He is also the author of the classic fantasy novel *The Secret of Dragonhome,* as well as installments in the Star Trek, Are You Afraid of the Dark?, and The Outer Limits series.

Mr. Peel currently lives just outside the New York Net, and will be 145 years old in the year 2099.